THREE-QUARTER TIME

A suspense novel by

K. Robert Campbell

Copyright 2024, K. Robert Campbell

ISBN: 9798325409738

Except for historical figures, all characters depicted in this novel are fictional. Any resemblance too any real person, living or dead, is purely coincidental.

Dedicated to the hundreds of musicians, actors and other denizens of community theater and musical groups that I have had to pleasure to work with over the years.

Published by Coastal Highlands Press

Other works by K. Robert Campbell

The Fifth Category
Cameron's week begins with a nightmare that portends the hornet's nest of betrayal and intrigue that awaits him when he takes on a new client.

The Fourth Estate
Cameron's working vacation becomes a deadly cat-and-mouse game when murderous thieves threaten his client.

The Third Degree
A woman keels over dead next to Cameron on a mountain train tour, and the police want to know why his name is on a slip of paper in her pocket.

Second Hand
A roaring tornado stays Cameron's argument before the State Appeals Court, leaving a dead judge, and a search for why he died.

First Class
Too many of Cameron's law school classmates are dying, and a common thread among the deaths leaves him worried that he's next.

Zero Tolerance
Cameron's potential new law partner has a missing client, and the search for her leads into a quagmire of shady people and shady dealings.

Twelve Tales: A Calendar's Worth of Cameron Scott Mysteries
Twelve short mysteries, each tailored to a month of the year, from January's 'A Dead Start' to December's 'Knitting Noel'.

THREE-QUARTER TIME

CHAPTER ONE

Dear Mr. Scott,

I think somebody's trying to kill our tuba player. I'll be very busy tomorrow, but if you can come to the Oktoberfest on Saturday, I'll give you the details. Please help.

Sincerely,

Philip

Attorney Cameron Scott re-read the note, trying to make sense of it. 'Philip' had scrawled it on the back of a music sheet, folded it, and clipped it onto a potted plant on Cameron's office porch. Cameron knew that receptionist Nedra had worked until seven the night before, so when she came in, he asked her if she had seen or heard anything unusual the previous evening.

Nedra said, "No. is something wrong?"

"No, no. Nothing's wrong. Or at least you didn't do anything wrong."

Cameron held out the note for Nedra. "This guy, Philip, left this pinned to the whatever-plant-that-is on the front porch overnight. I hoped maybe somebody saw him."

Nedra took the note from Cameron and muttered, "The plant's a fiddle-leaf fig," as she read it. She snorted and looked up with a grin, "The tuba player? Really? Do you think somebody's playing some kind of weird joke?"

"Might be a joke, especially since he pinned it to a 'fiddle' leaf something."

Cameron took the note back and asked, "Do you recall any clients in particular named 'Philip' that might be in a band? Not a rock band. Maybe some kind of big band or something."

"Not that I can think of. Do you want me to do a first-name alphabetical search through the client index?"

Cameron looked back down at the note. "Nah, don't worry about it right now. Have you heard about some kind of Oktoberfest thing going on around here?"

Nedra moved the computer mouse around and clicked, typed a bit, and quickly found an answer to Cameron's query. "Here you go. There's one up in Whittington on Saturday. Aren't they big on tubas?"

Cameron leaned over and looked at the website that Nedra had pulled up. "Looks like Mary and I might need to take a quick polka lesson."

With the note in hand, Cameron made his way to new associate Ken Benton's office. He knew that partner Ben Gravely would be at the courthouse until afternoon, and planned to talk to him later. Through Ken's open door, he saw him engrossed in a casebook. Knowing that if Ken did not want interruptions, he would have closed the door, he walked in and said, "Do you know anybody named Philip that plays in an Oktoberfest band?"

Ken set the book aside and said, "An oompa band? No, not that

I can think of. Why?"

"A what?"

"That's another name for a German fest band."

"And you know that how?"

"I played drums for an oompah band in my undergrad years. Lotta fun. Anyway, I don't know anybody who plays in a local German band."

"Do you know anything about the Oktoberfest this weekend in Whittington?"

"Oh, Yeah. It's been a yearly event in Whittington for about...I guess twenty years now. I don't know anybody in the band, but I'm going up to it with a date."

"Hmm. Mary and I might join you." Cameron handed the note to Ken.

Ken read it and handed it back, saying, "That's intriguing. What do you suppose it means?"

"I don't have the foggiest idea. This Philip guy took the trouble to clip this to our fiddle-leaf fern or fig, or whatever, on the porch, so I suppose we oughta look into it. Then again, It can't be too dire a problem if he can wait two days to see us. What time are you planning to go up there?"

"The fest starts at eleven, and I'm supposed to pick up Mia at ten."

"Mia. I've heard you talk about her a bit, but it'd be nice to actually meet her. I'll see if Mary wants to go up there with me. I'd like to see what this note is about."

"Great. I think you'll enjoy it."

♪

Mary agreed that an Oktoberfest could be something different and fun to do, so at about half past ten on Saturday, she and Cameron found themselves at the back of a huge, open-sided tent, trying to figure out how they would meet Philip.

At the front of the tent, the 'oompah band', as Ken had called it, sat on a raised platform. The band, about twenty strong, included two tubas, and Cameron wondered which tuba player was the purported victim.

Mary commented, "I love those German costumes. What do you call those fancy dresses–dirndles? And I can just see you in a pair of those leather britches."

"Can see me as in 'I'd look sexy in them', or as in 'you'd get a good laugh'?"

"I'm not saying. The hats are cool though." Most of the players wore fedora-type hats with feathers stuck in the hatbands and adorned with various decorative pins. Mary pointed to a wooden beer keg resting on a stand center-stage and said, "Do you suppose the musicians drink out of that?"

"Seems like they wouldn't be able to read their music after a while. Must be a prop."

A dance floor had been laid on the ground in front of the bandstand, but the rest of the tent was filled with rows of long, narrow tables lined up perpendicular to the stage and adorned with blue and white-checked tablecloths. People seated at the tables drank beer from steins of various shapes and sizes. Many of the people seated or milling around the tent also wore what looked like traditional German clothing. The rest were dressed the same as Cameron and Mary, in everyday casual outfits.

Cameron scanned the waiting crowd to see if Ken and his date had arrived, but could not pick them out from the sea of bodies in front of him. He prompted Mary to follow him into that sea, and they waded their way down an aisle between two rows of tables. When they got about halfway to the stage, a voice cried out, "Wilkommen, Herr und Frau Scott." Cameron turned to see Ken Benton seated at a table, waving. With his embroidered shirt, and a fedora, he fit in well with the crowd.

Cameron and Mary negotiated their way to Ken, who pointed to two empty seats on the opposite side, saying, "I saved those for you. I figured it'd be easier for us to talk face-to-face." The people seated at either side of the empty chairs smiled and waved at the Scotts.

When the Scotts got seated, Ken introduced their immediate neighbors first, and then turned to an attractive, dark-haired young lady next to him, saying, "This is Mia. Mia Schmidt."

Mary said, "Pleased to meet you Mia," and reached over to shake her hand.

Mia answered with a light German accent, "I am delighted to meet you as well. I have heard much about you and your husband from Kenneth."

Cameron also shook the young lady's hand and joked, "Kenneth's a lawyer, so be wary of what he tells you."

Mia laughed and responded, "So you're not as wonderful as he says you are?"

Cameron's face reddened a bit and he said, "That would be true only if he's talking about Mary. So, what part of Germany did you come from?"

"Actually, I'm from Austria. Bavaria, to be exact."

"Oh, sorry."

"That's perfectly all right. I know we all sound very much alike to most Americans."

Ken said, "That includes me. But Mia tells me that a Bavarian can easily tell if somebody else comes from another part of Austria, or from somewhere in Germany, depending on their accent. Kinda like we can tell a New Yorker from us."

Before anyone could say another word, a costumed man standing in front of the musicians shouted into a wireless microphone, "Are we ready to start this fest?"

The crowd responded, 'Ja' and held up their steins. The band leader repeated the question two more times, each response of 'ja' getting louder, and then the band launched into a song that started with "Ein Prosit..."

Ken leaned toward the Scotts and shouted, "That's a song that kicks off the fest. It's kind of like saying, 'A toast to the good times'."

When the song ended, the bandleader cried, "Eins, zwei, drei," and the crowd roared, "gsuffa!" after which they took good swigs from their beer steins.

The noise level decreased considerably when the band stopped, and as the band leader welcomed the crowd and engaged in further patter, Ken explained, "Okay, 'eins, zwei, drei' means 'one, two, three,' and then the word that sounds like 'zoofa' roughly means 'down the hatch'." He looked at Mia, who nodded her agreement.

Mary looked at the glass container in front of Ken and said, "Is that a pitcher?"

Ken laughed and said, "No, this is actually a beer stein. It's called a mass, spelled m-a-s-s, but with the 'a' pronounced 'ah'. There's a single German letter that substitutes for the two esses we use."

"Wow. That'd get you drunk fast."

"I tend to nurse it along all day. You'll see a lot of the band members do that too."

"That's good to know." Mary turned her attention to Mia. "So, how long have you lived in this area?"

Mia said, "About four years here in Riverport, but I have lived in the U.S. for fifteen years. When I was twelve, my father's company transferred him to Pennsylvania to help open a new plant. He's an engineer and they needed his expertise."

Conversation ended when the band launched into a polka song, and the group settled into enjoying the music. When they finished, Cameron said to Ken, "Let's get to a quieter place so we can talk for a minute."

Ken stood and told Mia, "Remember I told that Mr. Scott and I might need to talk business for a few minutes after he got here?"

Mia nodded, saying, "I understand. I'll talk with Mrs. Scott and our friends."

Ken led Cameron to a quiet area away from the tent, with few people around. Cameron said, "Do you have any idea which of the two tuba players our note-writer was talking about?"

"Not a clue. Turns out I know a couple people in the band, so I'll try to talk with them when they take a break. Meantime, I hope you and Mary can enjoy the music and the atmosphere."

"It's certainly different. Where did you get those–what do you call them–lederhosen?–you're wearing?"

"Lederhosen, yup. Literally 'leather pants.' Actually, mine are more correctly called kneebundenhosen, because they're knee-britches. I got them and the rest of the outfit online."

"Did all the pins come with the hat?"

Ken laughed. "I've collected these over the years at different fests." He took off he hat so that Cameron could see it closer. "Every October, there's a slew of fests that go on all over the place, and some of them not too far from here. Like I said, I played in a fest band in college, and I still get a kick out of them. Mia wants me to go to one in Pennsylvania some time."

Cameron said, "Speaking of Mia, I guess we'd better get back to our ladies. Be sure to let her know we'll be talking with the band at break."

"Will do. Want to get a beer?"

"I'll get one for Mary. You know I don't like to drink at all if I'm going to be driving, so I'll abstain."

"Like I said, I'll be nursing mine along all day, so I'm not too worried about driving home. Then again, Mia's stein is a lot smaller, so I may get her to drive home anyhow."

At the beverage vendor's tent, Cameron ordered a small souvenir stein of lager for Mary and a root beer for himself, and they threaded their way back through the crowd.

By the time Ken and Cameron got back to the table, the band was in the middle of a waltz tune. Instead of dancing, most of the people on both sides of the table swayed back and forth to the music. On

Cameron's questioning glance, Ken shouted, "That's called 'shunkeling'. He sat with Mia and she immediately linked arms with him to join in the swaying.

When Cameron sat, he put the stein in front of Mary and she said, "Thanks. Join in." She immediately looped her arm around his and got him into the rhythmic movement.

When the music ended, the crowd erupted into exuberant applause and the band launched into another 'ein prosit'. Steins became a little emptier. After a few more songs, the band leader announced that the band would take a short break.

Ken said something to Mia and stood. Cameron told Mary, "Work time. Ken and I are going to talk to some band members. Are you going to be okay?"

Mary said, "I've been having a great time talking with Mia and my new friends here, so take your time."

Ken made a beeline for the drummer, with Cameron in tow. Cameron said, "Why aren't you playing with this band?"

"For one, I sold my drum kit right after college. I knew I wouldn't have time to play during law school, and I needed the money. And I'm way out of practice now. The waltzes are in three-quarter time and usually a little more leisurely, but the faster stuff can sometimes get tricky. These three and four hour gigs can wear you down, too. I sure miss it though."

Ken flagged down the drummer before he had a chance to leave the tent. "Long time no see, Jeff. This is my boss, Cameron Scott. Cameron; Jeff Kelly."

Cameron shook Jeff's hand and said, "Good to meet you."

Ken said, "Jeff's a dentist here in Whittington, and he keeps my teeth in great shape. We've known each other for a while, but I never knew he was a drummer." To Jeff, he said, "I know your break's short, so I won't keep you long, but I need to know if there's anybody in the band named Philip."

Kelly said, "As a matter of fact, here comes one of our Philips right now." He pointed to a roundish-looking, gray-haired man in lederhosen scurrying toward them. When the man reached their side, Kelly introduced him, "Ken, Cameron, This is Phil Pritchard, one of our first-trumpeters."

Ken said, "Oh my gosh, Phil Pritchard. We were in a band together during my undergraduate years. How you been, buddy?"

Pritchard grinned and said, "Ken. Ken Benton? Holy cow. What've you been up to?"

"I went on to law school and wound up down here, practicing with this guy." He pointed to Cameron and introduced him to Pritchard.

Pritchard eyed Cameron and said, "I bet you don't remember me, do you?"

Cameron, racking his brain, said, "I'm afraid you're right. Give me a clue."

"It's been a few years back. You helped me get out of a speeding ticket."

"That has been a while. I quit handling criminal several years ago. Are you the Philip who left me a letter?"

Phil turned to Jeff and said, "Can you bring me a beer when you come back?"

Kelly took the hint and left for the beer tent. Phil then said, "Yes, that was me. Listen, can I get you to talk with Tuba John at our next break? He won't listen to me."

"This is the tuba player you talked about in your note? By the way, why didn't you just call?"

"Oh, yeah, sorry. I was on the way home from a practice. I knew I'd be tied up all day Thursday and Friday, and it just seemed easier at the time."

"That's okay, it worked. So, tell me about this tuba player."

"His name is John Westheimer, but we call him Tuba John He's been with the band since the beginning."

Cameron gave Ken an 'Okay by you?' look and Ken nodded

agreement, then Cameron said, "We'd be glad to talk with him."

"Good. I'll let him know and we'll talk with you next break. Right now, I gotta get back on stage."

When Pritchard left, Cameron started sniffing and said, "What's cooking that smells so good?"

Ken said, "That's the brats, uh, bratwurst. You need to try some. Usually comes with sauerkraut and German potato salad." He pointed to a nearby vendor tent. "Line's not long; let's get some.

They purchased two orders apiece and then rejoined the ladies. Mia and Mary were both delighted with the treat, and as they all started to eat, the band broke into another round of 'Ein Prosit' They then launched into a medley of fast polkas, ending with another 'Ein Prosit' and 'ein, zwei, drei, gsuffa'. Cameron asked Ken, "How often does that get repeated?"

Ken said, "A lot. Each time, the crowd takes another quaff, and soon, they're loosened up enough to get up and dance."

"I hope they can still stand on their feet, with all that zoofa-ing."

Ken laughed. "Believe it or not, there's usually not too much problem with people getting over-drunk. Most folks who come to a lot of these know how to handle their beer."

After a few more sets of songs and prosts, the band took another break. Cameron and Ken beelined for the bandstand. When they got there, Phil Pritchard met them, with John Westheimer in tow. John, a tall, stately looking man, appeared to be in his late sixties. After introductions, Westheimer said, "I appreciate you meeting with me. I think Phil here may be building it into something more than it is, but it did give me a start."

Cameron said, "What would 'it' be?"

"Oh, I thought Phil already gave you the details. We both belong to a concert band. That band plays about four times a year at Graves auditorium, over at the community college. Things get pretty hectic when this band is in fest season along with the concert band cranking up for a show. Anyway, at rehearsal at the auditorium the other night, a huge chunk of metal hit the stage right behind me. I don't know what it was or where it came from, but it scared the crap out of me."

Ken said, "Huge chunk of metal? What did it look like?"

"I dunno. Kind of a steel bar with a 'U' shape cutout at either end."

"Ah, a stage brick."

Cameron said, "A what?"

Ken explained, "It's a counterweight for balancing curtains and lightbars and stuff that go up and down on the stage. I guess they got the name 'brick' because that's kind of what they look like."

"And you know this how?"

"Because I also did stagehand work during college to help pay my tuition."

"How did you find time to study, between stagehanding and oompah-ing and I don't know what else?"

"Late nights."

Cameron said to John, "Anyway, you mentioned the, uh–stage brick–falling."

John said, "I chalked it up to being a weird accident. Maybe we'd let the management know and that'd be that. But our conductor got all bent out of shape and said she wanted to call the whole concert off. I told her she'd disappoint about sixty people who've been practicing so hard for a couple of months, not to mention the people who like to come hear us. That calmed her down, but she still insisted that we see the auditorium manager immediately after rehearsal, and moved me to another spot."

Cameron said, "What did the manager say?"

"He apologized and said he'd look right into it. He said nobody should have been on the rail at that time, since all the soft goods were already in."

Cameron looked to Ken for a translation. Ken said, "The rail's an elevated walkway where workers can move back and forth to raise and lower curtains–the 'soft goods'–and light bars and such.

Lowering them is called bringing them in and raising them is called taking them out."

Cameron nodded acknowledgment and asked John, "Where were you in relation to the 'rail'?"

John answered, "I usually sit stage left, with the other low brass–that's the left side of the stage when you're looking out at the audience. At that auditorium, the rail's overhead, on stage left. At the time, though, we were standing around waiting."

The fest band leader called the players to come back to the stage, so Cameron took out a business card and gave it to John, saying, "Give me a call at the office on Monday. I'd like to look into this a little more."

Ken said, "So, you think there might be more to it?"

"Maybe, maybe not. I'd like to get more information first. I'm hoping we can take a look around that stage. John, do you know the manager's name?"

"I think it's Mike. Mike Stevens, or something like that."

"Okay, I know you've got to go play, but give me a call first thing Monday and let's see if your friend Phil has any legitimate concerns. What kind of work schedule do you have?"

"None. I've been retired for two years now. I've got lots of other things to do, but I can always rearrange them to meet with you."

"Okay, talk to you on Monday."

John went back to the stage and Ken and Cameron headed back to the seating area. As they walked, Cameron spotted Phil Pritchard scooting over to Tuba John and having a quick word with him.

Ken and Cameron got themselves seated with their respective mates, and the band started into yet another 'ein prosit'. This time, Mary and Mia sang along, and both uttered a resounding 'gsuffa!' followed with a quaff of beer. The band leader asked, "Who's ready for a chicken dance?"

The tent erupted with a cheerful 'Ja!' People jumped up from their seats and rushed to the dance floor. Mary stood up and pulled at

Cameron's arm, saying, "C'mon." Cameron looked toward Ken for a way out, but Ken and Mia were already on their way to the dance floor.

Cameron managed to have a good time doing the chicken dance. He also danced a sort-of polka with Mary a few times until the end of the fest. Before they left, he said to Ken, "How about calling this Mike Stevens as soon as you can and arrange a backstage tour for us. Do your best to convince him that we're not suing the auditorium; we're only trying to figure out if somebody's trying to harm Mr. Westheimer."

Ken said, "Will do."

CHAPTER TWO

Around midday on Monday, Ken came to Cameron's office and said, "I got hold of the auditorium manager. He said they don't have anything going on tomorrow if we want to come in. You were right–I did have to convince him that we weren't planning a law suit."

Cameron said, "Hazard of our profession. I'll give Mr. Westheimer a call and see if he's available."

When Cameron called, Westheimer's answering machine kicked in, and Cameron started to leave a message, when a voice interrupted saying, "Hello?"

Cameron said, "Oh, hello, is this John Westheimer?"

"It is. I heard the phone ringing when I came in from the yard, but I couldn't get to it in time to beat the answering machine. Have you found anything out?"

"Not yet. Ken and I are going to the auditorium tomorrow to get more information, and I'd like you to come with us to let us know exactly where you stood, and so on. Can you meet us there at two?"

"Sure can."

"All right. See you there."

Cameron went back to Ken's office to let him know what time they would be going, and that Westheimer would meet them there. Ken called Stevens to confirm the time.

♪

On Tuesday afternoon, Cameron and Ken stood peering through one of three sets of glass doors at the auditorium's main entrance. Tuba John Westheimer waited with them. Precisely at two o'clock, a man walked across the spacious lobby inside to unlock the doors. By his neatly trimmed, graying hair and business-casual attire, Cameron judged him to be the facility manager. As soon as he got the door opened to let them in, he introduced himself, "Hi, I'm Mike Stevens. Which one of you is Mr. Benton?"

Ken said, "That's me." Pointing to Cameron he said, "And this is Cameron Scott, our senior partner."

Cameron shook Stevens' hand and said, "We've brought Mr. Westheimer, the tuba player from the concert band." Stevens raised an eyebrow slightly as he shook Westheimer's hand, but said nothing.

By the time introductions were done, another man had stepped through an open doorway opposite the entry doors. His bright orange-red hair stood out against his all-black outfit, and Cameron could best judge his build as 'thick'. Stevens motioned for him to join them and said, "This is my technical director, George Hall. The crew call him 'Trail Boss'." To Cameron, Stevens' tone seemed a bit dismissive when he mentioned the nickname.

Hall shook each of their hands and then Stevens pointed to the door from which Hall had made his entrance and said, "This way."

Everyone followed Stevens through the door, which brought them to the rear of a dimly lit seating area. As he looked down over the vast expanse of seats that raked downward to the brightly lit stage below, Cameron said, "It's been a while since I've seen a concert in here. How many does this place seat?"

Stevens swept his hand upward toward a ceiling about ten feet over their heads. "Including our balcony up there, we have about fifteen hundred seats, give or take a few. He led them down a walkway between rows of seats, out from under the balcony, where the sloping main ceiling of the room spanned about forty feet or more overhead.

They walked down until they stood at the foot of a stage that looked cavernous and plain without all its curtains and adornment. The back and side walls consisted of black-painted cinder block. The 'soft goods' hung suspended twelve feet up. All but the main curtain appeared to be heavy black fabric of some sort. Their full length extended another twenty feet or so up to what looked like an industrial steel grid. Cameron peered over a waist-high wall in front of him, into a sunken oblong area, and said, "I take it that this is the orchestra pit."

Stevens said, "It is. We seldom have musical productions here, but when we do, it comes in handy."

A set of stairs ran perpendicular to each end of the stage, and Stevens led them up the ones to their right. Cameron looked all around and his gaze rested on a row of vertical floor-to-ceiling ropes lining one of the sidewalls. He asked Stevens, "What do all those ropes on the right do?"

Stevens answered, "That's actually left. From up here, you call your directions as you're looking toward the audience." Cameron wondered if he imagined it, or did Stevens' response again have an air of haughtiness about it?

Cameron said, "Oh, right, Mr. Westheimer told me that. Tell me about that structure about, what...twenty, twenty-five feet up."

"That's the fly rail. It's actually twenty-three and a half feet up. When we need the pipes that hold curtains and lighting fixtures moved up or down, that's where it gets done."

"It looks like you have some of your counterweights–bricks I guess you call them–stacked up around the bottoms of the ropes there. Do you keep any of them up on that flyrail?"

"Most of them, actually. It's a very sturdy structure; well supported."

"Mind if we go up and take a look around?"

"Not at all. I hope you're not afraid of heights though."

"I think we'll be okay."

To Westheimer, Cameron said, "I want you to stay down here, and then let us where you were when the brick dropped, all right?"

"Okay."

Stevens turned to Hall and said, "You can go back to the shop now. We'll call you if we need you." Hall hesitated, but when Stevens glared at him, he skulked his way across the stage and through a set of double doors at the back.

Stevens took Cameron and Ken through a doorway at the right end of the rope array. They had to immediately turn left down a short hallway with white cinderblock walls and linoleum floor, and left again into a longer hallway. Cameron said, "The other side of this wall is where the ropes are, right?"

Stevens said, "Correct. The door down on your right takes you to the flyrail stairway, and through the door at the end there's a dressing room." He walked them to the stairway door and unlocked it.

The door opened to a small landing, at the foot of a long stairway that stretched up to their right. That stairway ended at a landing with a door to the right, and they made a u-turn to another, equally lengthy, set of stairs. As they started their climb, Stevens explained that the door led to a hallway with more dressing rooms. Ken said, "How many dressing rooms do you have?"

Stevens said, "Two here on stage left, and four on stage right; two right off the stage and two more on the second floor."

"Wow, we only had three all-told in my college theater. I remember they would get mighty crowded during a musical or dance recital or something."

"Did you get into some of your college productions?"

"Nah. I worked backstage my junior and senior years. We actually got paid for that."

"I guess everything back here looks pretty familiar to you then."

"It does. Only on a grander scale. The theater I worked in only sat about five hundred."

By the time they reached the top of the second stairway, Cameron panted, "I've got to catch a breather for a second. I didn't realize how much I've gotten out of shape over the years." He did not mention that his calves felt like fire.

Stevens said, "If you're not used to twelve-foot stairways, it can be a bit wearing." They stepped out onto a painted concrete floor with assorted pieces of what looked like old stage equipment lining the walls. About five feet in front of them, three steel steps rose to a small steel platform and a closed door. Cameron said, "Is the flyrail up there?"

Stevens said, "No, that's the rail for front-of-house lights." He did not elucidate, and Cameron figured he would get Ken to explain later. In the meantime, Stevens led the way to a different entryway to their right. He disappeared through it, and Cameron and Ken followed.

As soon as he got through the doorway, Cameron stopped so suddenly that Ken nearly bowled him over. Cameron said, "Whoa, it didn't dawn on me that we'd be looking straight down to the stage!" They had stepped onto the narrow, steel mesh flooring he had seen from floor level, with a long row of vertical ropes to their right. Steel safety rails lined both sides of the walkway. At waist-level, a long steel bar spanned the entire length of the walkway, with a steel lever in front of each set of ropes.

Stevens said, with a grin, "I guess I'm so used to looking down through the floor that I don't think about how jarring it must be to first-timers. Sure you want to walk out here?"

Cameron said, "I'll trust that the whole thing won't fall down because I'm on it now, so yes." He followed words with action and stepped, gingerly, onto the walkway, allowing room for Ken to join him.

On the steel-mesh floor, to his left and partly beneath the bottom guardrail, a row of thick metal blocks, stacked about five high, stretched toward the far end of the walkway. He asked Stevens, "Are those the stage bricks?"

Stevens replied, "They are."

"How much do they each weigh?"

"There's two kinds; whole bricks and half-bricks. The whole ones weight about forty-four pounds each, and of course, the half-bricks weigh about twenty-two pounds each."

"All right if I lift one?"

"Sure. Use your legs though. I don't want to see any back sprains."

Cameron slid what appeared to be one of the thinner bricks from a pile and lifted it. Stevens said, "The 'U' shape at either end lets it straddle the ropes." He unlatched one of the levers on the closest rope and told Cameron, "Pull this one down a few feet and then up a few feet."

Cameron put the brick back on its pile and pulled the front rope down. The one behind it moved up in tandem. A black curtain overhead moved downward a few feet. He pulled the rope back up and the curtain moved up. Stevens said, "See, it's not too difficult to pull the curtain up or down because it's counterbalanced with these weights."

Cameron looked at the piles of weights and said, "There sure are a lot of those things piled up here. Guess I shouldn't have been worried about adding my measly hundred-ninety pounds."

Stevens said, "If you can stand to lean over the rear guard rail a little bit and look straight down between the ropes–way at the bottom–you can see a lot of the arbors where all the weights are stacked up. We have to have enough to offset the weight of the curtains, as well as the bar they hang on."

Ken added, "It takes a pretty good stack of them to offset a lighting bar."

Cameron said, "I'll bet." He added, "I see you've got more

weights down at stage level."

Stevens said, "Oh yes. We usually pull the arbors up here to add them, but sometimes we need to put them on down there."

Cameron said, "Speaking of 'down there,' I 'bout forgot we left John down there. He called out, "John, you still there?"

A voice came up, "I am. What do you need?" and John moved into Cameron's line of sight.

"Go over to the ropes until you see a stack of metal weights. Some are thicker than others."

John came into view as he walked toward the ropes. He stopped and said, "Okay, I see them."

"Good. Tell me if those look like what fell behind you at rehearsal."

John leaned over to inspect the weights and said, "Yup. Exactly like one of those thinner ones."

"Okay, thanks. We'll be back down in a minute. No, wait. Let me get you to stand where you were when the weight fell near you."

John took several steps toward the front of the stage, and then moved a little further onto the stage. He hollered, "Right about here."

Cameron walked down the walkway to a spot even with where John stood and looked down at a stack of weights at his feet. He said, "Anybody up here have a flashlight?"

Stevens said, "Always," as he fished a small penlight out of one pocket. He handed it, lit, to Cameron, who played the beam on the weights.

Cameron asked Stevens, "Is there a way you can tell whether any of these bricks have been moved recently. Or, rather, whether any have been moved that shouldn't have been moved?"

Stevens said, "We haven't needed to move the ones at this end of the flyrail for a few months." He peered intently at the stacks and said, "I'd say a brick or half brick at the top of this stack got removed recently."

Cameron said, "How can you tell that?"

"The rest of them have a 'patina' of dust. This one doesn't."

"Good observation. Should anybody have been up here before the band started rehearsing?"

"Not once we got the soft goods in. Trail Boss—uh, George—needed some cleaning done in the workshop, so all hands were supposed to be back there with him."

Cameron looked down the flyrail, and spied a circular stairway at the far end. "Where does that lead?"

Stevens pointed up to a large steel-mesh 'ceiling' over their heads and said, "To the grid. Wanna go up? There's standing room between that and the upper ceiling of the building."

"I'll pass for now. Is that stairway the only way to the grid?"

Stevens pointed to an opening on the stage right wall that extended upward through the grid. The right wall of the opening had rungs embedded in it. "That's another entry, but we don't use it much, unless there's a special reason."

"And I take it the band had no special reason for its use."

"That's right."

Cameron hollered down, "Thanks, John. We'll be down in a minute." The three of them made their way off the flyrail and back down the stairs to the stage.

When they got back onto the stage, Cameron asked John, "How noisy was it on stage when that weight landed behind you?"

"Pretty loud. Lots of talking, and some of the players were already warming up their instruments."

"Did anybody look toward the flyrail when the weight hit the stage?"

"Hell no. Everybody was too busy gaping at the weight itself."

"Makes sense." To Stevens, Cameron said, "Mike, were you in the area when the brick hit the stage?"

Stevens replied, "I was in my office, off the balcony mezzanine."

"Did anybody notify you after it happened?"

"One of the stagehands called me on his cell phone."

Cameron asked John, "At the time, did you think that somebody had tried to hit you with the weight, on purpose?"

"Good heavens no!"

"Were all the band members accounted for at that time?"

"Best I could tell. I didn't do a head count or anything though."

"Anybody pissed off at you, that you know of?"

"I can't think of anybody."

Cameron looked at a deep divot in the wood stage floor. "I take it that the brick hit here."

Stevens said, "That's the spot. I grilled the crew about how it happened but far as any of them knew, none of the bricks have been moved for at least a month."

Cameron asked Ken, "Any questions for Mr. Westheimer or Mr. Stevens?"

Ken said, "John, do you know of anybody in the band who has a serious quarrel with anyone? Serious enough for someone to want to cause them harm?"

John said, "I'd have to ask around, but what would that have to do with that thing almost hitting me?" Cameron made a mental note of the divot's location, about six feet behind where Westheimer said he had been standing.

"Maybe somebody meant it to warn somebody else, or maybe even to hit somebody else. I don't know, but it's worth thinking about. Will you check on that? Discreetly, of course."

Cameron said, "Good point, Ken. Mike, we appreciate your cooperation. John, we'll follow up with you on...when do you think you'll be able to make your inquiries?"

"I can call a few of the band members I've known for quite a while, starting with Phil. Let's see...give me about two weeks, okay?"

"Two weeks it is. By the way, when is the concert supposed to take place?"

"Originally, next Friday night, but with the recent scare, and several band members coming down with flu, Mr. Stevens has agreed to postpone it to a month from this Wednesday."

Stevens nodded agreement.

Cameron said, "I'd love to come hear you, so I'll put it on my calendar. Thank you, gentlemen. John, let me know when you get more information, and Mike, let me know if you find out any more about what happened."

On the way back to the office, Cameron asked Ken, "What do you think?"

Ken said, "It doesn't look like we have much in the way of legal issues here. I mean, we haven't been hired by anybody to do anything; Phil Pritchard only asked us to look into it and John Westheimer hasn't asked us to do anything. Right?"

"I agree. But you've been around me enough by now to know that I don't like unanswered questions. That stage weight made its way to the floor somehow, and I don't think a poltergeist did it. I think somebody may still be in danger, and I'd like to do what I can to prevent them from being harmed, client or no client."

Ken sat silent for a while, and Cameron let him ponder. Finally, Ken said, "This isn't the kind of thing that came up in any of my law school classes. Even my ethics classes talked more about client confidences and conflicts of interest and stuff, but not anything like this."

"Ken, sometimes you just have to do what's right, and it doesn't have anything to do with whether you've been hired by someone, or whether some rule or law compels you to do it. At any rate, I don't want you to feel obligated to help; it's more of an inner drive for me."

Ken did not respond and Cameron changed the subject to some of the legal matters they had pending, until they arrived at the office.

At some time late in the afternoon, as Cameron concentrated on proofreading a client document, he saw some movement at his office door. Without looking up, he said, "Come on in, Ken. Have a seat."

Ken came through the door and closed it behind him before sitting in one of Cameron's client chairs. He cleared his throat and quietly said, "I haven't been able to concentrate on my work much since we got back. Mind if we talk?"

Cameron put the document he had been reading aside. "Not at all. What's up?"

"I've been thinking a lot about what you said. I'm not sure that's an ideal I could live up to, but I'd like to."

"You mean about doing right? Hell, I can't always live up to it myself. Mary lets me know that. A lot. It's not a strict rule; more of a good path to take whenever you can. You know, you had no obligation to help out when we got into that mess at the court of appeals, but you did. Whatever your reasons, you did the right thing. And that time when your aunt asked you to help the cousin you hardly knew. You weren't obligated to help, but I get the feeling something inside drove you to help her anyway."

"I guess I never looked at it that way. I mean, I didn't really think about whether I should have been involved, I just did it."

"That's what I'm talking about. You don't sit and make all these philosophical arguments with yourself; you act because your instinct says you should."

"Well, right now, my instinct is telling me that I should help find out why that stage brick fell. So tell me what I can do."

Cameron smiled. "You understand what kind of mess you could be getting into, right?"

"I've been with you on a couple of your exploits, so yes, I understand. And I want to help."

"Okay. I haven't even had time to think about it that much yet, but when I figure out what to do, I'll definitely keep you in the loop. Meanwhile, we need to get back to the work at hand."

Ken stood and said, "I appreciate it," before going back to his own office.

Cameron spent the rest of the afternoon catching up on his client work.

CHAPTER THREE

On his way home from work, Cameron listened to some of the day's news on his car radio. One story caught his attention: A suspicious backpack had been left at a mall in Charlotte, North Carlina, a little over four hours from Riverport. A bomb-sniffing dog had zeroed in on it, but a bomb squad found nothing but crumpled-up newspapers inside it. Police were conducting a thorough forensic search to see why the dog had identified it. At that point, no evidence had been found about the backpack's owner, and no-one had claimed it.

After dinner, Cameron told Mary that he needed to do a little research in his home office before settling in to watch television. He went straight to his computer and pulled up any information he could find about the bombing. Little more had been reported since the first story broke, but he did find that the crumpled newspapers were from a county not far from Charlotte.

Something about the newspaper name jogged Cameron's memory, and he did some more searching. After a while, he came upon a story from several months back in which bomb-sniffing dogs in Raleigh had hit on a suspicious pocketbook left in a school restroom. In that instance, someone had stuffed the pocketbook with crumpled newspapers from the same publisher.

Cameron closed down his computer and joined Mary in the den.

She said, "Whatcha been looking for? Client stuff you can't talk about?"

"No, I can talk about this. Did you hear about the bomb scare over in Charlotte today?"

"Backpack stuffed with newspapers or something? Yeah, we got a low-level alert at the plant." Mary, a control-room supervisor at a nearby nuclear power plant, often received such warnings.

"You know how my curiosity works–I wanted to check into whys and wherefores. Not much, except something in the story reminded me of a news report from a few months ago, up in Raleigh where they had a bomb scare at a school."

"Is there some kind of connection?"

"Maybe. Both times; a suspect package, stuffed with crumpled newspaper from the same small-town publisher."

"That's nice, but is there some kind of connection that you're involved in?"

Cameron laughed. "You know me too well. Probably no connection to anything I'm working on. More curiosity than anything. I am working on something that I can tell you about though."

"What's that?"

"It's not a client matter, per se, but something that's been brought to my attention. You know the auditorium out at the community college?"

"Uh-huh, Graves Auditorium. We've been there."

"We have, but it's been a while. The Fullwood County concert band had a rehearsal there the other night. Seems that their tuba player nearly got hit by a stage-weight that fell off an overhead catwalk."

"Anybody hurt?"

"Nobody hurt, but the stage got a pretty good dent in it."

"So, does somebody want you to sue over it or something?"

"No. I went out there and checked it out, but there's really nothing to sue over. It started when a band member who's heard of my, uh...exploits...asked for me to look into it."

"Oh brother." Cameron could almost hear Mary's eyes rolling as Mary continued, "You're not about to get yourself into another 'exploit' now are you? Because if you are, I want you to be sure your will is up to date."

"Very funny. No, I don't think there'll be anything more to it. But I am curious as to why the stage weight fell down like that."

Mary did not respond, so Cameron thought it best to change the subject. "So what's on tonight?"

They found a program they both liked and settled into watching television for the rest of the evening.

CHAPTER FOUR

On Wednesday, a packed schedule kept Cameron busy with client conferences until lunchtime. When he got a breather, he buzzed Ken to let him know that he hadn't had time to think about the stage-brick incident.

Ken responded, "I thought about it a little last night, but my ideas might sound a little dumb."

"Let's talk about them and see if they lead anywhere. Why don't you come to lunch with me at my house, and we'll talk about it there."

At the house, they sat in Cameron's home office with sandwiches and cold drinks. Cameron said, "All right, tell me about your ideas."

Ken took a long swig from his drink and then said, "like you said, a poltergeist didn't throw the stage brick down, so there had to be some sort of human, or maybe an animal, involved."

"Animal?"

"I suppose a large cat or something could have pushed it off. The pile that it most likely came off of had to be higher than the steel apron of the flooring, so there wouldn't have been a need to lift it."

"Still, that would have taken a mighty hefty cat to push a twenty-two pound block of steel off of the pile, wouldn't you agree?"

"Okay, maybe not a cat; maybe a raccoon or something. All we know is that nobody from the staff was up there."

"We don't know that for a fact. We only have Mike's word for it. Or rather, he has his technical director's word for it. Mike said he was up in his office at the time."

"I hadn't considered that. Do you think we should go back and talk to some of the backstage staff?"

Cameron paused for a bit to think. "Yes, but here's another thought. With Mike in his office and the staff in the shop, that would have left the stage completely unattended for at least some period of time before the band arrived. We need to confirm whether that's true. Do you know anybody who works there?"

"Sort of. Seems like I've heard Mia mention knowing the lighting person. Want me to follow up on that?"

"Yeah, let's see if we can talk to somebody who would have been in the workshop during the cleanup. When can you get up with Mia?"

Ken pulled a cell phone out of his pocket and said, "I can call her right now if you want."

"Isn't she at work or something?"

"She manages a gift shop in town, so yeah, she's at work."

"I wouldn't bother her with a phone call. How 'bout sending her a text and let her answer when she can."

Ken tapped the message into his phone and said, "Done."

By this point, they both had finished eating, and they headed back to the office to tackle their respective workloads.

Later in the afternoon, Ken stopped by Cameron's office. "Mia says the lighting person's name is Sheila Rivenbark. She wasn't sure of her number, but said she'd get it for me as soon as she could today."

Cameron said, "Okay, thanks." Ken turned to go but Cameron said, "Before you go, let me ask you something."

Ken turned back around and said, "Shoot."

"Seems like I remember lots of florescent lights all the way at the top ceiling of the stage, above the mesh gridwork. Do I remember right?"

"What we call the grid-lights. That's what lit our way up there. They get shut off during productions, but they provide plenty of light for whatever stage work needs to be done."

"Would you normally look up there without a specific reason to do so?"

"Hmmm. No, I suppose not. Usually, when you're working on stage, you're looking around the stage or the floor, and even when you go to the flyrail, you're usually looking at the ropes and curtains, or down at the stage. I don't recall ever looking up to the grid area without a good reason."

"What would be a reason to look up there?"

"Well, for instance, you might have watch while somebody drops a line to attach rigging for suspended speakers."

"Does that happen often?"

"Usually when rock bands come in, but I can't think of many other times. Why?"

"Wondering if somebody could sort of 'hide in plain sight' up there without being noticed."

"Ooh, good thought. I have no idea."

"Okay, well, let me know when Mia gets that number to you."

"Will do."

Ken went back to his office and Cameron plowed into the mound of paperwork on his desk.

Late afternoon, Ken buzzed Cameron with the phone number that Mia had obtained. He said, "She also had the number for a stagehand–Paul Franklin. Want to call now, or are you still swamped?"

"A stagehand's who we need, so let's try that number. I need a break anyway, so come on down."

Ken came to Cameron's office and settled into a chair. Cameron called Franklin's number first, and somebody picked up on the third ring. Cameron said, "Hi, am I talking with Paul Franklin? I'd like to go to speakerphone if you don't mind, so my associate can also hear. Is that okay? Good. Hold on a second."

Cameron switched the speaker on and continued, "Mr. Franklin, I'm Cameron Scott at Scott and Gravely law firm, and my associate is Ken Benton. We're looking into why a stage brick fell from the flyrail where you work. We talked with Trail Boss the other day and he mentioned that the crew was cleaning up in the shop when the brick fell. Do you know if the stage was left unattended at some point before any of the band members got there."

Franklin said, "Yeah, Mr. Stevens told me about your visit. I think we got done sweepin' the stage and bringin' in the soft goods at about four that afternoon, and the first band members got there around five, so yeah, as far as I know, it would have been unattended."

"And to your knowledge, nobody else came through the shop toward the stage?"

"No, we'd have noticed that."

"Not even somebody saying they had some band equipment to deliver, or something like that?"

"Wait a minute. You know what? One guy did come in early with a cymbal case. Said it missed getttin' on the truck and he had to get it there early for the percussion section."

"Did you see where he left it?"

"Can't say that I did. I guess we all got busy cleaning and figured he went on out to the stage."

"All right, Mr. Franklin, you've been a great help. If you would, hold on for a second and let me see if Mr. Benton has any questions."

Ken shook his head 'no' and Cameron said, "He doesn't have any questions, so I'll let you go now, thanks."

"Okay, g'bye."

Cameron hung up and looked at Ken with eyebrows raised. "Looks like we need to see who this delivery person might have been. Do you have your friend Phil Pritchard's number?"

"I've got it somewhere in my desk. Do you want me to get it and come right back?"

"Nah, we've done enough for today. Let's make that call tomorrow."

CHAPTER FIVE

First thing Thursday morning, Ken told Cameron, "I got Phil's number. Let me know when you want to make the call."

Cameron said, "No time like the present. Let's go to your office."

Ken called Phil and asked, "Hey, Phil, Do you recall who brought cymbals in early for the band rehearsal last week? Really? So, you don't know if anybody else dropped off some equipment early? Ok, thanks. Nah, we're checking some leads is all. Bye."

Ken hung up and said, "According to Phil, all their equipment comes in one truck, including the drum equipment. He doesn't recall anything being left off the truck. Players bring their own horns and stuff, but nobody needed to make an extra delivery that afternoon."

Cameron said, "Hmm. I wonder who came in with the cymbals? Maybe we need to call Paul Franklin back and see if he can give us a description. I'll take care of it when I get a chance today."

"Okay, and–" Ken's phone rang. "That's Phil calling back. I guess I should answer."

Cameron nodded and Ken picked up. "Hey, Phil, what's up? No kidding? Okay, I'll pass it on to Cameron, thanks."

When Ken rang off, Cameron asked, "What?"

"Phil says he remembers there being an extra cymbal case backstage when they packed up to go. He hadn't seen it before and nobody owned up to bringing it. It only had a couple of cheap hi-hats in it wrapped up in a bunch of newspaper, so they threw it in the truck anyway."

"You don't need to call him back right this second, but when you get a chance, let him know to keep the case and cymbals intact. Something tells me that at some point, it might need to be dusted for fingerprints."

"Really? Sounds like you've got a theory brewing."

"Nothing solid; only a few random ideas competing with each other. What did Sherlock Holmes used to say? 'Never theorize until you have all your facts.' Or something like that. Okay, let's get to work."

Cameron went back to his office, but found it hard to focus on his work. Fortunately, his workload for the day was light, so he closed his door, hit the 'do not disturb' on his phone and sat back to think. He mulled over some ideas for a while, but got nowhere, and finally picked up his phone and called partner Ben.

Ben answered, "Hey, what's up?"

"Got a few minutes? I want to toss a few ideas around with you, and I need your criminal mind. Let me rephrase that–I need your knowledge of criminal matters."

Ben laughed, "Sure glad you corrected yourself. You need me right now?"

"Yeah, if you're not too tied up."

"Be right there."

Within a minute, Ben came in and took a seat. Cameron said, "I've got something gnawing at me and I need to toss it around with you; make sure I'm not getting too far afield in my thinking. You've worked with me longer than Ken, and you know a little more about how my mind works, so let's see what you think."

"I don't know if I should feel complimented or worried."

Cameron laughed. "Probably both. Here's the thing. Ken and I have been checking out something that happened over at Graves Auditorium the other day. We don't exactly have a client at this juncture—"

"Oh no, not another one of those."

"I know, I know, seems like some of our non-client 'cases' have brought on the most trouble. Anyway, it started with a note clipped to the fiddle-leaf plant out on the front porch the other day. The county concert band's playing at Graves Auditorium soon, a heavy metal weight smashed down behind their tuba player during a rehearsal one night, and the note writer's afraid somebody's trying to kill the guy."

"Wait a minute, back that one up a little bit. A note?"

"Yeah, the guy who left the note—turned out to be the drummer for the band—got worried. I did a closing for him a while ago and—"

"And he's heard about your crazy exploits."

"Well, I guess that might have come into play. Anyway, a twenty-two pound bar of steel used as a counterbalance for the curtain system dropped from an overhead walkway, about twenty-five feet up. It bounced off the floor about six feet behind the tuba player."

"I guess that would be cause for concern. Have you been over there to check it out?"

"Ken and I both went there. Turns out Ken's had some experience working backstage at a theater, so he translated a lot of stage jargon for me. There doesn't seem to be any clear reason for the weight to have dropped. Management swears that none of the employees would have been on the walkway at that time, and for all anybody knows, it might have been something precariously balanced that chose that moment to fall."

"But you don't believe that."

"Nope. I think somebody knocked it off, although not necessarily on purpose. But, like I said, everybody who works there seems to be cleared."

"Any idea of who it might be then?"

"One possibility. Somebody said that a mysterious delivery person brought a cymbal case to the auditorium on the day of the rehearsal. He came in when the crew was busy in the workshop behind the stage, and the manager was working in his office off the balcony mezzanine. But, the band's drummer tells us that a truck carries all the band's percussion equipment and other heavy stuff."

"Who talked to this delivery person?"

"One stage hand, who told him to leave the case on the stage. We're going to follow up with him to get a description, but I get the feeling he won't remember much. Nobody remembers seeing the guy come back through the workshop after that, although they may have been too busy or too distracted to notice anyway. The drummer says they had one more cymbal case after practice than they came in with, so yes, somebody did really come in with it."

"Is there another way out of the building from the stage?"

"Plenty, if you head toward the lobby. Exit doors on either side of the seating area, as well as the rear exits to the lobby."

"So, whoever brought the cymbal case in could have taken one of those exits, right?"

"That seems most likely, but I've still got nagging questions of why he came in claiming to make a delivery, and why a twenty-two pound weight suddenly decided to drop out of the air."

"I see where you're going as far as the potential for a deliberate assault or some other crime, but surely you don't need me to confirm that for you."

"No, you're right. But there's something else." Cameron paused.

"What is it?"

"This is the part where you tell me if I'm going too far afield. Okay, I've seen recent reports about backpacks or other containers being left where crowds gather, sniffer dogs hitting on them, but nothing but crumpled up newspapers being found inside. I can't help but feel that there's a connection, somehow."

"Whoa, that is out of left field. Sounds kind of like putting one and one together and getting fifteen."

"It does, doesn't it? But you know how my mind works,

especially the back of my mind. So humor me. In your criminal cases, have you come across any talk about backpback bombers or something similar?"

"Funny you should mention that. Last week, another defense attorney was down here on a case, and we got to yakking over lunch. He said he had to defend a student once who allegedly left a backpack full of explosives in a school hallway. Somebody got suspicious and they brought the dogs in. Didn't take long for them to hit on the bag and it got taken out before it could blow up."

"What happened to his client?"

"His fingerprints were all over the backpack, but not on any of the explosives. He admitted to owning the back and said he brought to school with him every day."

"Did they find him guilty?

"Without his prints on the explosives, the DA couldn't get beyond a reasonable doubt and they found him not guilty. Here's the weird thing; somebody hid the explosives in crumpled-up newspapers."

"Did he say where this happened?"

"Umm, I think he said Kannapolis, but I could be mistaken."

Cameron paused. "Kannapolis?"

"I'm pretty sure, why?"

"Remember I said how those other packages had nothing but crumpled newspapers inside?"

"Yeah?"

"Both times, the newspapers were parts of the Cabarrus Citizen Times, and Kannapolis is in Cabarrus County."

"Whoah, that's spooky. Not sure how that ties in with your flying stage weight, but I'm sure you'll tell me."

"This is where my thoughts get a little nebulous, but there might be a connection. You know that cymbal case I told you about?"

"Uh huh."

"All it had in it was a pair of cheap hi-hat cymbals, wrapped in

-37-

newspaper."

Ben's eyebrows shot up. "Holy crap, Cameron. Now I see where you're going. What newspaper?"

"We don't know yet. The band still has the case on their truck as far as I know. Let me get Ken in here." Cameron picked up his phone and buzzed Ken's intercom number. "Can you come on down to my office? I think it's time to call Phil again."

When Ken got seated, Cameron said, "Ken, I told Ben about the mysterious cymbal case and the disappearing deliveryman. Our discussion led to a question that might lead to an unsettling answer, so I want you to call Phil and find out where the band keeps its truck. I'll fill you in on the details when you find out."

Ken took out his cell phone and rang up Phil, saying, "Hey, Phil, can you tell me where the band keeps that truck with all the band's equipment in it? I don't know, Cameron's asking about it. Okay, shoot." Ken scribbled an address on a slip of paper Cameron had slid over to him, and said, " 'Preciate it Phil. Talk to you later." When he ended the call, he gave Cameron a questioning look.

Cameron quickly filled Ken in on the conversation he and Ben had about the newspaper-filled containers, and then made a call. "Elliott, don't you have a bomb-sniffing dog in your K9 corps? Good. I've got a job for him. I'll fill you in when we get there." Elliott–Sheriff Grainger–arranged to meet Cameron with a deputy and the dog at the address Ken had taken down. Cameron ended the call and then told Ken, "I need you to call Phil one more time and let him know that somebody who can open the back of that truck needs to meet us there in twenty minutes."

Ken said, "Will do," and started redialing Phil's number.

With a grin, Cameron said to Ben, "I know you don't want to get involved in 'one of my messes', as you like to put it, so thanks for the info and I'll let you know what happens."

As Ben started out the door, he said, "Now you've got me intrigued, so yes, do let me know."

Ken got off his phone and told Cameron, "Phil says he has a key to the padlock and can meet us there."

Cameron said, "Great. Let's go." When they got into Cameron's truck, Cameron said, "I don't think we have an explosives situation on our hands right now, but I figured it's time to bring Elliott in on this." Sheriff Elliott Grainger, an old acquaintance of Cameron's, had been involved in some of his past cases. Cameron had seen him rise from Deputy to Chief Deputy to Sheriff, and they had an ongoing mutual respect for each other.

Elliott, a deputy with the sniffer dog, Ken, Cameron, and Phil all arrived at the truck's location within a few minutes of each other and Phil unlocked it, asking, "What are we looking for?"

Ken said, "That cymbal case you told me about."

Elliott took out a pair of rubber gloves and handed them to Phil, saying, "Put these on before you touch that case, okay?"

Phil said, "I'm starting to get a little nervous." He looked toward Ken for an explanation.

Ken said, "You're not in trouble, and it's nothing drastic, but we need–" He looked toward the Jack Russell terrier at the deputy's side and at the deputy.

Elliott said, "This is Deputy Bohn, with Lucky."

Ken continued, "We need to let Lucky here sniff around that cymbal case."

Phil nodded and started moving some equipment around. "Are you thinking there might be some drugs in there?"

Elliott said, "Not necessarily," but added nothing else.

Cameron said, "Do you need help?"

Phil shook his head. "Nah, the drum equipment got loaded in last, so it shouldn't be–ah, here it is." He leaned over a kettle drum on the left side of the truck and pulled up a round black canvas case. He handed it down to Bohn, who already had a pair of gloves on, and climbed back down to the ground. "Need me to keep the truck open?"

Elliott said, "Yes please."

Bohn held the case by its handle and directed Lucky to smell it. The dog sniffed all around it, but made no sign that it detected anything. Bohn then unzipped the case and let Lucky sniff the inside. The dog at first backed away a little, but did not otherwise react. Bohn reached inside and gently pulled out the paper-wrapped cymbals. Lucky sniffed and whimpered, backing away a little, but still did not give a 'hit' signal. Finally, Bohn removed the papers and let Lucky smell the cymbals themselves. This time, Lucky sat immediately. Bohn said, "It's the cymbals."

Ken said, "Whew. Smells like somebody's been doing their laundry."

Elliott said, "Let him smell the inside of the papers, where they touched the cymbals."

Bohn did as directed and Lucky let out a short bark as he sniffed, but turned his face away.

Cameron said, "Deputy Bohn, could I look at the top of one of those pages?"

Elliott nodded his okay, and Bohn held the paper up for Cameron, who took a quick look and said, "That's what I suspected."

Elliott said, "What's what you expected?"

"The newspaper is the Cabarrus Citizen Times."

Elliott said, "I know you'll tell my why you suspected that." To Bohn he said, "Let's repack it send it to the lab. We want to confirm what Lucky hit on, and get everything dusted for prints, and whatever else they can find."

Phil held the cymbals, case, and papers, while Bohn took Lucky back to his car and brought back a large black evidence bag. Phil said, "I'll tell you right now, my fingerprints will be all over those cymbals. I'm the one that checked out the case to see what was in it. You'll probably find other band members' prints, too."

Elliott said, "Duly noted."

While Bohn packaged the evidence, Elliott asked Cameron, "Mind telling me what this is all about?"

"I'm not absolutely sure, but I've got a hunch."

"Oh, hell, you and your hunches. I get the feeling we're in for a heap o' trouble. So tell me about it."

Cameron filled Elliott in on events since the note had been left at his office, and added, "My hunch is that somebody's been experimenting with ways to interfere with dogs' sense of smell. You might get the lab to check the outside of that paper for anything unusual."

"I think I see where you're going with this. If a sniffer dog can't smell what's in the package, anything could be in there, including explosives, right?"

"Exactly."

"Any ideas on who's experimenting?"

"None yet, but I'd send word out for K-9 handlers to watch out for suspicious packages that smell like bleach."

"Bleach?"

"When that cymbal case got opened, it smelled like a laundry room, and I seem to remember that bleach interferes with a dog's sense of smell. They don't like it."

Elliott raised an eyebrow. "Good point. I'll get the word out."

"Try not to make it too public. I don't think we want to alert whoever's experimenting that we're on to them. At least not yet."

"Okay. Any idea why they picked this place to try it out?"

"That, I'm not sure of right now. Maybe we can talk to Mike, the manager, about whether anything big's supposed to happen here in the near future."

Cameron took out his cell phone and called Mike's number. "Mike? Cameron Scott. When would be a good time for Sheriff Grainger and me to stop by and talk with you? Hang on, I'll check."

He asked Elliot, "Tomorrow at one-ish work for you?"

Elliott paused for a moment while thinking and then said, "Yeah, I can do that. Over at the auditorium?"

Cameron said, "Yup," and got back on the phone to confirm the

-41-

time with Mike. When he ended the call, he said, "I guess we're done here for now. Thanks Phil." He thanked Deputy Bohn and told Elliott, "See you tomorrow," before motioning to Ken to head back to the pickup truck to leave.

On the way back to the office, Ken said, "What in the world is somebody from Cabarrus County doing down here testing out ways to fool a dog's nose?"

Cameron said, "Good question. I guess it's in Elliott's hands now, but I'd still like to know what's going on. Hope he lets us know what the lab finds out. Meanwhile, let's get some office work done."

CHAPTER SIX

At home Saturday morning, Cameron slept in past nine. When he awoke, he hit the bathroom first, then shuffled down the hall to the kitchen. Mary sat at the kitchen island, coffee cup in hand. She said, "Just made a fresh pot. I've only been up for about fifteen minutes."

Cameron grunted a reply and made his way to the coffee maker to pour a cup, then ambled to a stool next to Mary. He reached over and gave her thigh a light pat, said, "Mornin'," and then sugared his coffee. After a few languid sips, he said, "How'd you sleep?"

She took a sip before answering, "Probably no better than you. I tossed and turned all night."

"Same here. I think at one point you'd slung yourself sideways across me. I woke up another time with one arm and one leg hanging off the bed. Sheets are a tangled mess. Looks like we had a wrestling match."

Each of them drank more coffee before Cameron got up to start pouring himself a bowl of cereal. He hesitated for a moment, box in hand, and then said, "I'm in the mood for bacon and eggs. How 'bout you."

"You cooking?"

"Yup."

"Sounds good to me."

Cameron reached up and unhooked an iron skillet from an

overhead rack, and set it on the stove. Mary pulled a carton of eggs and a package of bacon from the refrigerator and set them on the counter.

As Cameron busied himself pulling off slabs of bacon and putting them into the skillet, he said, "I had the weirdest dreams. Don't remember all of them, but the one right before I woke up got pretty vivid. You were in it...sort of. I mean, it was you, but it wasn't you, know what I mean?"

"I think so."

"Okay, I was married to the other person and all, but she didn't exactly look like you. Actually, she started out blond, then went to dark hair somewhere along the line. And our house wasn't this house. Then I was in the car, driving somewhere out west, and then–"

"Is this going to be long?"

Cameron laughed. "It's hard as hell to explain a dream to somebody else, isn't it? There doesn't seem to be any rhyme or reason to what goes on. At least in most of my dreams there isn't."

"Same here. I think the only people who have linear dreams are characters in movies and television."

"Some people say that dreams are your subconscious trying to sort things out." Cameron paused for a moment. "Which might be true in this case. One part of that dream stands out in particular."

"What's that?"

Cameron turned the bacon over. "As I drove, somebody popped up in the middle of the road, telling me to detour to the right, when I could see a clear road straight ahead."

"Was he wearing a day-glo vest?"

"Ha. No, but his outfit looked familiar. Can't think of where I've seen it before, though."

"Probably a client or something."

"Yeah, probably. Anyway, it seems like my subconscious tried to tell me something." Cameron broke some eggs into a bowl and stirred, then took the bacon out of the pan and laid the pieces on a paper towel to drain. He turned down the heat and poured the eggs into the pan.

Mary said, "So, what's on our agenda for today?"

"Not a thing. Wanna go somewhere? Or is this a good sit-around-and-read day?"

"I'll go with door number two. I'm close to the end of the book I've been reading, so this would be a good day to finish it."

"This would be a good day for me to clean out my workshop."

Having satisfactorily planned their itinerary, they ate breakfast and spent the rest of the day as planned, until evening. They had a late supper, again eating at the kitchen island. In the middle of it, their land-line phone rang. They let it go to messaging, but listened as the caller spoke two words: "Back off," followed by a brief pause before the call ended."

They both stared at each other for a moment. Mary said, "What the hell was that about?"

Cameron stood, saying, "I don't know, but let's see who left it." He hurried into his home office to punch the phone's 'recents' button while looking at its message screen. No caller's name showed, but a phone number with a '513' area code appeared. Cameron pulled out his cell phone, quickly looked up the locale for that area code, and found it was for the Cincinnati, Ohio, vicinity. He went back to the kitchen to let Mary know the location.

Mary said, "I can't think of anything job-related for me that would come out of Cincinnati, how about you?"

"Not that I know of. I'll ask around the office on Monday though."

After supper, Cameron went back to the land-line phone and replayed the message to record it into his cell phone.

CHAPTER SEVEN

On Monday morning, Cameron stopped in to see Ben and Ken in their offices, but neither of them knew of any transactions with anyone from the Cincinnati area. He checked with receptionist Nedra, and she had nothing to add. No-one in the office had any record of a call that had come in from the number shown on Cameron's home phone. He went back to his office to dig into his pending work load until about mid-morning, when he pulled out his cell phone to listen to the message again. Before playing it, he buzzed Ken and asked him to come down to his office.

When Ken arrived, Cameron said, "I want you to listen to something and see if anything sounds familiar to you. It's not long, so I'll play it a couple of times."

Ken said, "Is this connected to that Ohio number you asked about?"

"Yeah. See what you think."

Cameron played back the recording from is cell phone a few times and asked, "Anything?"

"Nothing at all. You say this came through your land line?"

"It did."

"So, do you think it's somebody you know, playing around? I mean, they didn't call your work number here, right?"

"Good point. But I still don't know anybody in Cincinnati, and neither does Mary. And we haven't given our land-line number out to many people. Of course, it could have easily been a wrong number."

"But you don't believe that."

"Not really."

"Want to play it again on speaker and turn it up so we can hear if there's background noises?

"Good idea, let's try it."

Cameron turned the volume on his phone to maximum and replayed the message a few more times while he and Ken listened intently.

Ken said, "I think I picked up on something. Play it one more time."

Cameron leaned in toward the phone when he hit the 'play' button and looked at Ken after the message ended. "I think I caught that, too. A faint noise in the background, almost like some kind of music."

"That's what I thought, too."

"Too short to identify, though. But the caller's voice sounded vaguely familiar, even though they tried to disguise it."

"I had the same impression."

Cameron put his phone back in his pocket and said, "I don't guess we're going to get much further for now, so let's get to work. I'll keep trying to figure out why they used my home number. And who the hell would have my unlisted number anyway?"

After Ken went back to his office, Cameron got an idea, and texted Mary, *"Rack your brain and see if you can think of anybody who would have our land-line number."* After that, he dug back into his day's work load.

At home that night, Cameron mentioned to Mary that he and Ken had listened to the message several times, and that they had detected what sounded like a short bit of far-off music in the background. She said, "Why don't we listen to the original message?"

They went to the home office, where Cameron turned the phone volume to maximum, and ran the message a few times. After the last run, he said, "Well?"

Mary drummed her fingers on her chair's armrest before answering, "Let's try it one more time."

Cameron ran the short message once more, and quietly waited for Mary's response. She inhaled deeply and exhaled slowly. Finally, she said, "I don't recognize the music, but can you find out what selections the concert band's supposed to play? Whatever's playing seems to be in three-quarter time."

Cameron cocked his head. "I think I see where you're going. I'll make some calls tomorrow morning. Meanwhile, let's go see what's on television."

"First, tell me about the text you sent me, asking about strangers who would have our land-line number. Is that connected to the 513 area code thing?"

"It is. I couldn't think of anybody we knew from there, but I wanted to double-check."

"I couldn't think of anybody either. I even checked the index in my cell phone, and nothing came up."

"Okay, well it was worth a try. Now, it's television time."

CHAPTER EIGHT

Cameron's Tuesday schedule stayed fairly busy until mid-afternoon. On his way to record some documents at the courthouse, he dialed Phil Pritchard and asked, "Phil, do you have a playlist for the band's upcoming Concert?"

"Yeah. I mean, I don't have it memorized, but I can get it for you. What's up?"

"Following up on some ideas about our mysterious flying 'brick'. Think you can text me a copy?"

"Sure can. You want it sent to this number?"

"That'll be good. No huge hurry; get it to me whenever you can."

"Okay. I should be able to send it after I get home tonight."

"Thanks. Talk to you later."

After Cameron recorded his documents at the courthouse and did some real estate title research, he decided to run by the auditorium, which was only about five minutes from the courthouse. He had no idea what he would expect to learn, but had a few thoughts in the back of his mind.

Cameron by-passed the front entrance and drove to the loading area behind the building. There, he saw a box truck backed in to the loading dock with its rear roll-up door open. Although the bay door behind it also stood open, he saw no activity around it. He pulled into a parking spot and walked up the ramp toward the bay. At that point, he spied two workers in black outfits with headsets on, leaning against a rail, smoking. He introduced himself and one of them gave his name as Paul Franklin. Cameron shook his hand and said, "Good to meet you. We talked on the phone the other day."

Franklin nodded. "Oh yeah, I remember." He turned to the other smoker and said, "This is Billy Twyford. He's a part-time stagehand, too. 'Sup?"

Cameron shook hands with Twyford and said, "Good to meet you, too. I'm following up about that brick that fell off the flyrail. I don't guess anybody has remembered anything else peculiar about that day, have they?"

Twyford replied, "I'm not sure who all was here that day. I know it had to be the TD and Mike, 'cause they're the full-timers. Them and our box office manager, Jodie. Everybody else is part-time, like me and Paul. They call us when there's a gig happenin', like the ballet thing tonight."

"What's a TD?"

"The technical director. He's our backstage boss, and then Mike's his boss."

"Jodie—was he here the night the brick fell?"

"She. Jodie Miller. Wanna talk to her?"

"Sure. Is she here?"

"I think so. Lemme check." Twyford pushed a button on his headset and said, "Hey Greg, you know where Jodie's at? Can you ask her to come out to the dock? Thanks." He told Cameron, "She usually doesn't wear a headset when we're loadin' in. Greg's gonna tell her we need her back here."

"Thanks."

Twyford cocked his head for a second, then pushed the headset button again and said, "Will do." Twyford told Cameron, "Gotta go. We got work to do." He and Franklin both extinguished their cigarettes and hurried inside.

Within a few minutes, a young lady with shoulder-length, mousy-brown curly hair strode from the workshop. As opposed to the other workers, who wore all black, she wore blue jeans and a light blue, long-sleeve shirt. She nodded at Cameron and then looked around nervously.

Cameron said, "Are you Jodie?" She focused on him and nodded.

With hand outstretched, Cameron introduced himself and said, "Billy said you manage the box office here."

"That and whatever odd jobs they need me to do. What can I help you with?"

"If you have a few minutes, I'd like to ask a few questions."

"About what?" Jodie kept glancing toward the shop, and Cameron noted that her voice seemed a bit shaky.

"I'm not sure if anybody has told you, but I'm an attorney and I'm trying to follow up on an incident that happened here the other week. I don't represent anyone who's trying to sue the auditorium, but I am concerned about the safety of people who come here."

"Okaaay. I guess you're talking about the lamp that blew out?"

Cameron tried not to register any surprise. "Well, that, and the falling stage brick. Why don't you tell me about the lamp first."

"I'm not sure I'm supposed to talk about these things, but everybody here knows about the F-O-H overhead that blew out the other week."

"F-O-H?"

"Front of house. You know, lights in the ceiling over where the audience sits."

"Ah. Did anybody get hurt?"

"Luckily, we had an empty house. The crew was settin' up risers on stage and we all heard a loud 'pop', and then glass came flyin' down all over the middle of the front rows of seats. First time that's ever happened, and I can tell you, it was pretty scary."

"I'll bet."

"Probably won't happen again, 'cause we're gettin' all LEDs put in next week, while we got nothin' booked."

-51-

"That's good to hear." Cameron made a mental note to ask auditorium manager Mike about that incident. "Do you know about–"

As if on cue, Mike's voice sounded from the doorway. "Housekeeping got everything shipshape?"

Jodie let out a quick gasp, then regained her composure before turning to Mike and answering, "I think so. I know they cleaned and vacuumed around the seating last night, after the conference."

"You know we don't 'think so'; we need to know so. Why don't you go ahead and double-check."

"Sure thing." Cameron could not quite interpret the look on Jodie's face as she turned to go back inside; something between fear and defiance.

Mike said, "Sorry about that, but we have a lot to do for tonight. Probably would be best to give me a call next time, if you need any more information."

Cameron took the hint. "Will do, thanks." As he left, he wondered what Mike didn't want him to know.

Back at the office, Cameron stopped at the front desk for messages. Nedra handed him a note that had only a phone number and the words *'call tom. betw.4-6 pm.'* He gave her a questioning glance.

Nedra said, "A woman just called. Wouldn't tell me her name and didn't want to go to your answering machine, but said she needed to talk to you."

"But doesn't want me to call until tomorrow?"

"Yeah, sorry, I didn't have time to write it all out before you came in."

"No problem. Guess I'll give her a call before I go home tomorrow. That it?"

"Pretty quiet otherwise." Nedra placed a stack of documents on the counter. "Here's stuff for you to review."

Cameron picked up the stack and said, "Thanks," on the way back to his office. After he reviewed the paperwork, he buzzed Ken's office and said, "You busy?"

Ken said, "I've got a few minutes. What's up?"

"Got a couple of theater questions for you. I'll be right there."

Cameron took the paperwork back to Nedra and said, "Everything looks good. I'll be in conference with Ken for a bit."

At Ken's office, Cameron settled in and Ken said, "What's new?"

"I made an impromptu stop out at the auditorium this afternoon. They were setting up for an event tonight, but I got to talk with box-office manager Jodie Miller, for a few minutes. Let me ask you, what would make an FOH light blow up all of a sudden?"

"Learning the lingo, I see. Normally, the lights over the audience aren't quite as high wattage as the stage lights, but they're still pretty high powered. Or at least they are if they're incandescent. I know that you can't change the lamp in a stage light without wearing gloves or holding it with a piece of cloth, and best I remember, you're supposed to do that with the overheads in the seating area as well."

"Why's that?"

"Any little bit of finger grease that gets on the lamp gets super hot and can screw it up. Sometimes they blow out and sometimes they kind of melt down. LED systems have their own problems, but that's not one of them."

"So, if somebody installed a bulb over the audience seating without using a glove or cloth, that could make it blow out eventually?"

"Could. I take it that they had a blowout at the auditorium. Is that what you talked with Jodie about?"

"Didn't intend to, but she volunteered the information. I didn't get to ask her about the brick, though. Mike kind of snuck up on us and told her to get back to work."

"Snuck up?"

"Yeah. I talked to her on the loading dock, near the open bay door. Mike kind of materialized out of nowhere. I could tell it startled

-53-

her, and maybe even scared her."

"Really? Why do you think it might have scared her?"

"He didn't say much, but I caught a bit of a menacing tone in his voice."

"Whoah. What in the world?"

"I don't know. But Nedra says a woman called this afternoon, apparently some time after I talked to Jodie, and didn't give her name. The woman wants me to call back between two and four tomorrow afternoon."

"And you think that might be Jodie?"

"Very good likelihood. I guess I'll find out tomorrow."

"So, where do you think this is all going?"

"No idea, but it doesn't look good. As usual, we don't have much information to take to law enforcement. All the same, it doesn't feel right."

"I know what you mean. I'll keep my eyes and ears open."

Cameron stood and said, "That's all we can do for now, I suppose." He looked at Ken's wall clock. "Ooh, I've got a four o'clock coming shortly. Bye." He headed back to his own office in time to talk with his client.

CHAPTER NINE

Wednesday's appointments occupied Cameron's time until mid-afternoon, when he got a break. He closed his office door and called the number that Nedra had given him the day before. The phone rang several times, and Cameron was about to hang up when a voice came on with a tentative, "Hello?"

Cameron responded, "Hi, this is Cameron Scott. I had a message to call this number between two and four today. How can I help you?"

He recognized Jodie Miller's distinctive voice. She said, "Oh yes, Mr. Scott. Thanks for callin' back. I'd like to talk with you–in private, if that's okay."

"Certainly. I can see you here at the office if you'd like."

"That would be great. Do you have an opening tomorrow? I'm off all day."

Cameron looked at his desk calendar. "Tomorrow at...let's see...any time after three would work."

"Perfect. How about three-thirty."

Cameron made a notation in the calendar while he said, "Three-thirty it is. See you then."

"Okay. And thanks for lettin' me talk with you."

Jodie ended the call, leaving Cameron wondering why she would use the term, *letting* me talk with you.' He shrugged it off, thinking he might be letting his imagination get ahead of him. In the meantime, he immersed himself in the work he had remaining for the day, and then went home.

By the time he got home, Cameron got a notification on his cell phone that Phil Pritchard had left him a message. He opened it and saw a complete playlist for the band's upcoming concert. Mary was not due home until six, so he busied himself pulling out ingredients to start cooking supper while he studied the playlist.

A song that caught Cameron's eye was "The Old North State." He knew it was North Carolina's state song, but had never heard it played anywhere, and was not familiar with its tune. He alternated between juggling ingredients to put in a frying pan with searching on his phone for a playable version of The Old North State. Finally, he found it, and set his phone down while it played, so he could start cooking the chicken breasts. About mid-song, as he was flipping the chicken, a passage caught his attention. He put the tongs down and replayed the song.

As Cameron was listening to The Old North State for the third time, Mary came through the door. She said, "That's pleasant. What is it?"

"That's our state song. I've never heard it played before. Anything sound familiar?"

Mary listened intently as Cameron ran the song one more time. "Oh me. That's what we heard on the mysterious phone message, isn't it?"

"I think so. After we eat, let's listen to the message again to be sure. Meanwhile, why don't you scout out some vegetables to go with this chicken."

"Smells good. I think we've got some lima beans in the freezer, and I'll grab a can of green beans from the pantry."

After supper, Cameron and Mary retired to his home office to listen to the phone message on the land line. After it played, Mary said, "Okay, let's hear that song again."

Cameron replayed The Old North State on his cell phone and at one point Mary said, "Yup, that's it."

Cameron said, "I'm going to text Phil and ask if he remembers what time they rehearsed that song." He followed words with action and then said, "What's good on television tonight?"

"I think they're having a Jeopardy championship on prime-time. Wanna watch?"

"Sounds good to me."

Midway through the program, Cameron's phone buzzed. He looked at the screen and said, "That's Phil. Let's see what he has to say."

Phil's text read, *"We had to work out some problems with ONS, so it was the 2d one we rehearsed that night. Prolly around 7:15 or so. 'Sup?"*

Cameron answered, *"Trying to coordinate some info, thanks,"* hoping that Phil would not press for details.

Fortunately, Phil answered with, *"Glad to help,"* and nothing further.

Cameron told Mary, "Be right back," and went to his home office. He punched a few buttons on the land line until he found the time that the threatening call had come in: 7:17. He went back to the den to let Mary know what he had found, and said, "I think we know where the call came from, don't we?"

Mary said, "Sort of. Do we know if they were rehearsing at the auditorium or elsewhere?"

"Good point. I don't want to bug Phil again, 'cause he might start asking questions. I'll wait and see if Ken can find out tomorrow. Seems kinda odd that they'd be rehearsing on a Saturday, though. I'll ask him about that. Meanwhile, let's see how many...or, more likely, how few...of these Jeopardy answers we can get right."

CHAPTER TEN

Thursday morning, Cameron waylaid Ken on his way into the office and asked him to find out where the concert band had rehearsed on Saturday, and whether it was odd for them to rehearse on a Saturday night.

Ken said, "I can answer both of those questions right now. They rehearsed at the auditorium. They don't usually practice on Saturdays, but it's the only time they could book the auditorium for a final rehearsal. I ran into Phil Pritchard yesterday afternoon and he gave me an earful about it."

"Final rehearsal? For a concert that's a month away?"

"The Governor's office said that next Thursday is the only time he can come down."

"Wait. What? How's the Governor fit into the equation?"

"You didn't know? Governor Danford's coming to the concert because his niece plays first clarinet in the band. They're playing the state song in his honor.'"

"Ah, 'The Old North State'. Mary and I identified it playing in the background on that threatening call we got. That explains why it's in the lineup. I suspect Elliott already knows that the Governor's coming, but I'll call him today abut the possible relation to our mystery cymbal case. Thanks for the info."

"No problem."

They both went about their business and when Cameron had caught up with his morning's work, he called Elliott at the Sheriff's office. "I guess you know the Governor's supposed to come for the concert next Thursday. After what we and the K-9 found out, is somebody trying to talk him out of it?"

Elliott said, "Mmm hmm. His people said he's got the utmost confidence in our law enforcement folks and the security folks he'll have with him."

"Seriously?"

"Seriously. They don't seem to think here's any real threat. And that's that."

"Hard to believe."

"Remember that Senator Randall's running against him this year. It's close to election time, and Randall's a real macho type. If Danford cancelled, Randall'd challenge him about how he'd face a real threat."

"Ugh, politics. It's all about public perception, isn't it?"

"You got it. Anyway, we've already got extra deputies scheduled, and a K-9 on call. Of course, there'll be several state troopers there, too. That's about all we can do."

"Okay, well, if I get any more information that sounds suspicious, you'll be the first to know."

"Appreciate it. Talk to you later."

"Bye."

Cameron hung up, musing about how ridiculous politics can get. He quickly decided that he had more important things to think about for the moment, and went back to his work load.

At 3:30, Nedra buzzed Cameron to say, "Ms. Miller's here for her appointment."

"Thanks, Nedra. I'll come up for her."

Cameron greeted Jodie and brought her back to his office. When they settled in, he said, "I'm glad you're here. I still have some questions I'd like to ask."

Jodie said, "Thanks for seein' me. I've got some questions too. I wanna know if I'm in any legal trouble."

"Legal trouble? What makes you think you're in legal trouble?"

Jodie hesitated, fumbling with her untucked shirttail. She looked around the room a little bit, and finally said, "Mike and me kind of have a thing goin' on."

"Oh. Well, that's a surprise. Why don't you tell me what kind of 'thing' and how that came about?"

"I guess it just kinda happened. I started workin' at the auditorium about five months ago, after Gus quit."

"Gus?"

"Yeah, Gus Danford. He was the box office manager before me."

"Do you know why he quit?"

"I don't know the whole story, but I think he had a squabble with our lighting director, Sheila Rivenbark. Mike...Mr. Stevens...wouldn't help settle it."

"Did it seem like the kind of thing Mike should have gotten involved in?"

"From what I understand, Gus and Sheila constantly butted heads over politics. I heard from some of the backstage crew that Sheila rode Gus all the time 'cause he's got the same last name as the Governor, and he'd get pissed, then she'd say "just kidding." I think Mr. Stevens asked her to back off, and she did for a while, but then she got worse."

"Any idea whether Gus actually is related to the Governor?"

"I don't really know, but they tell me he'd get pretty hot under the collar when she rode him."

"Hmm. Okay then, you're his replacement. How have you gotten along with Ms. Rivenbark?"

"She's a part-timer and I usually don't have much reason to talk to her, you know? The few times I've had to talk with her, she seemed to be okay. I mean, she's real territorial about 'her' light board, but I stay away from that anyway."

"Okay. Now, tell me how your 'thing' with Mike got started."

At this point, Jodie's faced flushed pink. She collected her thoughts and said, "We had to work together a lot, especially when I first started, and he had to show me how this auditorium's box office system works. Then, when things weren't that busy and we both got caught up with our work, we sometimes would sit in his office and yak. We found out that we had a lot in common. I'm not sure exactly how it came to this, but there's a couch in his office, and a lot of times he'd come sit on it while we talked. We wound up sitting closer and closer together until, well, we started kissin'. And then one thing led to another..."

Sensing her discomfort, Cameron said, "I understand."

Jodie said, "Anyway, that's why I'm afraid I could be in some kind of legal trouble, him bein' my boss and all."

"Are either of you married?"

"I'm not. I mean, I was, but I've been divorced for three years. The thing is, I found out the other day that he **is** married."

"I see. Well, as far as him being your boss, no, you're not in legal trouble. On the other hand, he could be, if you wanted to claim harassment. Outside of legal problems, your personal problems could get out of hand, especially if the other employees find out...or figure out...what's going on."

"Oh, we've been very careful about everything. I don't think anybody else would know."

"You'd be amazed at how the rumor-mill works at any place of business, especially one as close and personal as your auditorium. But this business about him being married–did you not have any clue about that?"

"He doesn't wear a ring, and nobody at work ever said anything about him being married. And his wife has never showed up at work any time I've been there."

"I think his wife would probably be your biggest legal threat, and that would be on the civil side rather than the criminal side. She could sue you for alienation of affections or even what's called 'criminal conversation,' which is another way of saying you had adultery with him. I know emotions often overrule good sense, but my advice is for you to stop this relationship, even if it means quitting your job."

Jodie's eyes were saucers. "Oh my God, even if I didn't know he was married in the first place?"

"That might be a defense you could offer. But now that you know he's married, there wouldn't be any defense if you don't break it off."

Jodie sat in stunned silence for a moment, then said, "Thank you, Mr. Scott. I had no idea it could get so complicated. What do I owe you?"

"Consider this a preliminary visit, with no charge."

"Are you sure?"

"No charge this time, but if you don't follow my advice, your next lawyer visit could get very expensive."

"I sure do appreciate it. Believe me, the last thing I want is an affair with a married man. Next time I work, I'm gonna let him know that our relationship has to be purely professional, or else I'm outa there." Um, there is one more thing."

"Okay."

"Well, I know you've been lookin' into that fallin' stage brick, and with the Governor coming next week and all..." Jodie looked at the floor for a while. Cameron waited. Finally, she said, "Promise you won't tell anybody I said this?"

"What you say will be treated as a client confidence."

"Well, my office isn't that far from his, and once, I overheard him on the phone talking about how much he hates the Governor and he sure hoped Randall beat him this year. He sounded pretty worked up about it. I just wanted somebody to know that in case somethin' happened."

"Thanks for telling me that. Let me ask you something. The other day, when we were talking, you seemed scared to death when Mike showed up. If you've been having a 'thing,' why were you so

-62-

scared?"

"I thought he was pissed to find me talkin' to you; afraid that I'd tell you about him and me, you know? Or maybe that he'd be jealous. He's got a really bad temper."

Cameron recalled the circumstances at the time and said, "So you think that's how he expressed his worry about being found out?"

"I guess so. Like I said, he's got a terrible temper, and who knows what he'd do."

"Okay, I guess that clears that up. I hope you give some serious thought to what I've said."

Cameron saw Jodie out, and went back to his desk to make a few notes about the visit. One of his notations made him pause to think. On a separate notepad, he jotted down *'check Danford/Randall feud.'* He next walked down the hall to see if Ken was in his office. The door was open and Ken sat at his desk alone, looking over some paperwork. Cameron said, "Got a minute?"

"Sure. What's up?"

Cameron settled into a chair in front of Ken's desk. "I just had a conference with Jodie Miller."

"Remind me who she is."

"The box-office manager at the auditorium. She called me and wanted an appointment."

"Really? What about?"

"Turns out that she and Mike Stevens are having an affair. Now she's worried she'd be in legal trouble over it."

"Over screwing her boss? Not that I know of."

"Me either, but there is a hitch–he's married."

"Oh. Possible alienation and all that, huh?"

"Yeah. I warned her about that, and she promised to break it off. But that's not what I wanted to talk about. Something she said during the interview caught my attention. She's only been working there a couple of months, and it looks like her predecessor quit over some political harassment from a co-worker."

"That's not terribly surprising, the way politics have been going these days."

"True. But the former employee's name really caught my attention: Gus Danford."

"As in Governor Danford? Think there's any connection?"

"Maybe. That's what we need to find out. He quit because the lighting director kept giving him a hard time about his name. According to Jodie, Gus complained to Mike, but Mike wouldn't do anything about it, so he quit."

"How does all that fit into our investigation?"

"Considering that the Governor's coming to the concert, I'd like to see how deep the animosity goes with this lighting director. I want to see if Gus might be available for a chat."

"Do you want me to check on that?"

"Nah, I'll handle it. But I'll probably want you in on the conversation, so let me know some times that you'll be available."

Ken flipped th rough his calendar and gave Cameron a run-down of available times and Cameron jotted them down. Before he left he added, "She brought up one more thing. According to her, Mike's got a pretty bad temper and he also hates the governor, so we should keep that in mind."

"Definitely."

Cameron then went back to his office to make some calls. First, he phoned Phil.

Phil answered, " 'Sup Mr. Scott?"

Cameron said, "Hey, Phil. Quick question. How many of the auditorium staff do you know?"

"The ones we deal with when we have concerts, for the most part. We don't see them much otherwise. Although... now that I think of it, one of them plays drums, so he and our drummer Jeff talk a lot."

"Ah, Jeff Kelly, right? I met him at the Oktoberfest."

"That's him."

"Would you happen to have his phone number?"

"I've got a roster of band numbers, so I can get it pretty fast. Can I call you back?"

"Absolutely." Cameron gave him his cell number and Phil said that he would call right back.

Within a few moments, Phil called with Jeff's number and asked, "Still working on the 'ghost of the opera house' case?"

Cameron laughed. "That's a good way to put it, yeah. Checking loose ends and stuff. Thanks for the number."

Cameron next called the number that Phil had given him. An automatic answer came on, "Jeff here. Leave a message," and Cameron left his number. At that point, Nedra buzzed to let him know that a client had arrived for an appointment, so he turned his attention to his business for the rest of the afternoon.

CHAPTER ELEVEN

Mary Scott had a late work schedule, and Cameron knew she would eat at work, so he threw a meal together when he got home and settled in to watch local evening news. One report covered the Governor's pending visit for the concert, and rumors of a threat being made. A reporter spoke with a representative of the Governor's office, who stated that "Threats against the Governor have become rather 'routine' under the current political climate. We take each threat under advisement, and the Governor's executive protection detail stays on alert, but we cannot allow the Governor's office to become paralyzed by unsubstantiated reports."

"Poli-speech at its finest," thought Cameron.

In the middle of the weather report, Cameron's phone buzzed, and 'Jeff Kelly' showed up on the screen. He answered, "Hi Jeff. Glad you called."

Jeff said, "Phil said you wanted to talk with me."

"Yeah, still trying to figure out how that piece of steel nearly obliterated your tuba player. Phil says that you've had a lot of conversations with somebody on the auditorium staff that plays drums. Do you mind telling me who that is?"

"Not at all. His name's Billy Twyford. I keep trying to talk him into joining the band, but he always says he's too busy. I know he has a day job at a car repair place, and the auditorium job is part-time, whenever he can get loose, so I understand."

"Oh yeah, I talked with him the other day. Would you happen to have his phone number?"

"Sure, hold on a second." The phone clicked and then went silent as Jeff looked through his contacts list, then he came back on and gave Cameron the number.

Cameron wrote the number down and thanked Jeff. He then called Twyford. "Billy Twyford? Cameron Scott here. We talked at the auditorium the other day."

"Oh yeah, the lawyer guy."

"That's right. Listen, I'd like to talk with you about something that happened at the auditorium recently. Anything we'd talk about would be strictly confidential, of course."

"Am I in legal trouble or somethin'?"

"No, no. Nothing like that. Still trying to figure out why the stage brick fell off the flyrail. I have a few questions about your lighting director and the former box office manager."

"Danford and Rivenbark? Yeah, they was like cat and dog."

"So I understand. Do you know much about Gus Danford?"

"I liked him and all, but we weren't best buddies or nothin' you know. He's kinda weird."

"I'm mostly interested in whether he's related to Governor Danford."

"Oh yeah. Sheila always ragged on him about bein' the Governor's nephew, or somethin', but that's all I know about it. She wouldn't lay off and he got pissed."

"Do you know anything about whether he complained to your manager about it?"

"One time, he told me that he bitched to Mike, but Mike didn't seem like he cared, so he was gonna quit. I told him he oughta take a chill pill and ignore Sheila, but he kept gettin' madder and madder about it."

"Does he still live in the area, or did he move away?"

"I'm pretty sure he still lives here. I see him every once in a while when I'm out. He always asks me if the bitch is still workin' at the auditorium."

"You wouldn't happen to know how to get hold of him, do you?"

"I think I still got his number in my phone. Hold on a minute and I can get it for you."

Twyford came back in a few moments and gave the number to Cameron, who said, "I appreciate it."

Twyford said, "No problem. Anything else?"

"No, you've been a good help, thanks. Talk to you later."

"Okay, later."

Cameron ended the call, and dialed the number given to him by Twyford. A 'leave your number' message came on, and Cameron left his name and number, stated his reason for calling, and then settled in to watch some television.

Mary came home a little after ten, and she and Cameron spent some time catching up with events of the day. They had barely settled in to watch the news when Cameron's phone buzzed. He did not recognize the number, but it had a local area code, and he surmised that it must be Danford calling him back. He answered and a voice said, "You the lawyer?"

Cameron said, "This is attorney Cameron Scott. Who am I speaking with?"

"This is Gus. I got your message. I kinda got the idea of why you're calling, but I don't know if I can help you any."

Cameron said, "I guess we can find out. Is there a time this week convenient to you to come to my office?"

"Well, um, right now I'm still looking for another job, so any day's fine."

Cameron took out the availability list he had gotten from Ken and recalled the gaps in his own work week and said, "How about tomorrow morning; say, eleven?"

"Sure, tomorrow at eleven's as good a time as any."

Cameron gave him directions to his office and said, "Thanks for agreeing to talk with me. I don't expect to tie you up for long."

"Okay, see you then."

Danford ended the call and Cameron said to Mary, "Did you detect anything unusual about his voice?"

"Except that he sounded a little shaky, no."

"Same here. Well, let's see what develops tomorrow."

They watched the late news and weather and headed to bed.

CHAPTER TWELVE

Appointments and document reviews filled Cameron's time for the first two hours Friday morning. At eleven, Nedra let Cameron know that Danford had arrived, and Cameron went to the lobby to greet him.

Danford's unkempt appearance struck Cameron immediately. Although his jeans and shirt appeared to be high-end brands, numerous wrinkles and a musty odor ruined the intended effect. It looked like he'd attempted to use a comb, but the hair on the back of his head looked like an abandoned bird's nest. Danford's adolescent complexion belied his real age, which Cameron judged to be late twenties or older. His breath, not particularly odious, smelled of stale cigarette smoke, as did his clothes. His red-streaked eyes darted around the room furtively. Oddly enough, he had a firm handshake and steady gait as he preceded Cameron to his office.

As soon as they settled into their seats, Danford said, "I know I look a mess, and I apologize. I stayed up late last night and wound up sleeping in 'til 10:30. I swear I'm not on drugs or anything."

Cameron laughed and said, "That's all right. This isn't a job interview. I have a few questions about your last job, and that's it."

"You mean the one at the fast-food place?"

"No, the auditorium job. I take it you went from that to fast-food. I did that part-time in my early college years, and it helped pay some bills, but I didn't find it too enthralling. Is that what you're doing now?"

"Nah. My idiot manager didn't have any idea what he was doing. I knew more than him about the job, and I had a lot of good ideas about how they could do things better, but he wouldn't listen. I think he was afraid that I'd take his job from him, so he fired me when I missed work one day."

"Out sick?"

"Something like that."

"Hung over," thought Cameron. He said, "Tell me about your box-office job at the auditorium. I understand you and the lighting director tied into it a few times?"

"Sheila? Yeah. Bitch wouldn't leave me alone about my Uncle Phil being the Governor."

"So he actually is your uncle. How did she know about you being his nephew? Did she assume it because of your last name?"

"Nah, I told her. I mean, it's not like I just came out and blabbed about it, but she kept blowing me off when I'd give her tips on how to light the stage better, and I let her know about my uncle, so she wouldn't think I was some bum off the street or somethin'. Know what I mean?"

"Did you have training as a lighting person, or work in the position before?"

"No, but it's an easy job, if you know what you're doing. But you have to have an innate talent for it that she didn't have, so I tried to help her out."

"I see. I forgot to ask–do you have a college degree?"

"Almost. I finished three years, but I got bored with it. I mean, after a while, it all gets repetitive, you know? I think they keep telling you things you already know so they can keep you longer and charge more tuition."

"I see. Well, tell me, what kind of things would Sheila say to you about being the Governor's nephew?"

"Enough to make me hate that I told her. Not so much about me as about him, really. She'd say he's corrupt, or a bully, or whatever crap his enemies dish out. And she'd tell me every stupid joke she read about him on line. I got tired of it. Mike wouldn't do anything about it, so I quit. 'Course, I didn't know I'd lose my other job so fast, so I'm in a mess now. Know anybody who's hiring?"

"Not at present. Have you heard anything about Mr. Stevens hating your uncle?"

"Mike? Nah. I mean, he's not overly fond of him, but I wouldn't say he hates him. Or at least as far as I know. We really didn't talk politics much."

"Okay, one more question. Would you have any idea how a stage brick could have fallen from the flyrail, short of somebody purposely dropping it?"

"Oh, I heard about that. Almost hit a tuba player or somethin'. That happened after I quit, so I don't know anything about it. Then again, the way they had those things stacked, it probably wouldn't take much for somebody to bump one by accident and knock it off, 'specially a half-brick."

"Has that happened before?"

"Not while I worked there, but somebody said it did happen a couple of years ago. They said it fell on a stagehand's shoulder and hurt him pretty bad. I guess he got worker's comp and they hushed it up, 'cause I didn't see anything about it in the papers or anything."

"All right, thank you Mr. Danford. If any more questions come to mind, would you mind if I called you?"

"No problem. Here, let me give you a number. It's at my parents' house. That's, uh, where I'm living for the time being." Danford's face reddened a bit as he imparted the information about his living arrangements.

Cameron saw Danford out and then texted Ken. *"Let me know when you're free, and we can talk about my interview with Gus Danford."*

Ken texted back immediately, *"Lunch. 12:30?"*

Cameron replied, *"OK"*

♪

Over lunch at Pelican Grill, Cameron outlined his discussion with Gus Danford, and the impressions he took from that talk. "He strikes me as a serial job-changer. Thinks he knows more than everybody around him, and doesn't hesitate to give his opinion, without ascertaining whether it's right or wrong. Either quits when nobody agrees with his words of wisdom, or pisses off the wrong people and gets fired."

"I've seen plenty of those types. Represented a couple in wrongful-termination suits, in fact."

"Did you win?"

"No. They had shaky grounds for the suits. The employers actually offered to settle, to make them go away, but they'd gotten so fired up about how 'right' they were that they wouldn't take my advice to settle."

"Self-destructive and clueless make a bad combination. Danford's all that, and it looks like he's got an alcohol problem to boot. But, I guess we can eliminate him as a suspect on the falling brick problem. It happened after he quit. I want to check him out a little more, but I'm not sure that he's a threat to his uncle. The only person I haven't talked to is the lighting director, Sheila."

Ken paused for a moment, thinking. "You know, I forgot that you wanted me to ask Mia about knowing Sheila. I'll talk to her about that tonight."

"Good. We need to find out as much as we can before next Thursday. In fact, call me as soon as you can after you talk to her."

"Will do."

♪

A little after seven o'clock, Ken called Cameron at home. "Got some news from Mia," he said. "Apparently, she met Sheila

Rivenbark a couple of years ago during a community theater production. Mia had a minor part, and Sheila did the lighting."

"Paid or volunteer?"

"Volunteer. She wasn't working at Graves auditorium yet, and was learning how to do lighting 'on the job' during the production."

"Did she have a full-time job at the time?"

"Uh huh. Ready for this? She worked for Danford's campaign team. Once he got elected, the job ended, but she thought she'd get a permanent position with his cabinet."

"And that didn't happen."

"Nope. Mia says that the way Sheila talked, she singlehandedly got him elected, and was super pissed."

"Did Mia find out why Sheila didn't get hired?"

"Indirectly, I suppose. Mia says that Sheila didn't work well with others. She'd talk down to the campaign volunteers, and second-guessed the manager constantly, even about matters that had nothing to do with the area she volunteered in. She also bragged to other people a lot about her 'connections' with Danford."

"Why do I get the feeling that Danford probably barely knew her."

"Right? Mia says that she almost quit the show, but decided to stay because the director was so good."

"I need to pass this info on to Elliott. She definitely sounds like a candidate for the watch list."

"I agree."

"Okay, Ken. Thanks for the update. Say 'hey' to Mia for me. You two need to join Mary and me for dinner some time."

"I think she'd like that. She and Mary really hit it off at the fest."

They ended the call and Cameron immediately dialed Elliott to give him the news about both Sheila Rivenbark and Gus Danford.

Elliott said, "Nothing too concrete on either of them, but enough to keep an eye on them, as far as the Governor's visit. Anything else new?"

"Not much since last time we talked. I'm trying to figure out how I can get a chance to talk with Ms. Rivenbark and see what vibes I can get."

"Vibes? Are you going into psychic research now?"

Cameron laughed. "Maybe. Nah, but I do want to see if she's really as hateful as she's been described. If I get to talk to her, I'll let you know the results. I guess the security plans are in high gear."

"They are. And since you and Ken are so familiar with the backstage stuff, I want you both unofficially on the team. I'll get all the clearances in order."

"Oh, well. I hadn't thought of actually taking part, but I'm honored to be asked."

"I know how you've dealt with situations like this, partner. I don't always agree with your methods, but you can sometimes get doors open that we can't for various reasons, if you know what I mean."

"Sure do. I'll let Ken know that he's going to be 'deputized' without being deputized. What time do you want us there on Thursday?"

"Doors open at seven and the concert's supposed to start at seven-thirty, and I've confirmed that the band is supposed to get there at about five to set up and rehearse. The Governor and his crew are supposed to get on campus at six-thirty or so. What say you and Ken plan to get there around two, if that's okay with you."

Cameron pulled out his pocket calendar and penciled the time into it. "Got it on my calendar. Let me know if anything new comes up."

"Same with you. Later."

When the call ended, Cameron called Ken back to let him know about Elliott's request, and the need to clear their calendars. He told Ken that he would work with Nedra in the morning to adjust their work calendars. After making a few notations at his desk, he went to the living room to catch Mary up on all the developments.

Cameron and Mary chatted for a while, and then they each settled into reading a book before retiring to bed.

CHAPTER THIRTEEN

On Saturday morning, Cameron drove to the auditorium, hoping some of the staff would be there. He hoped to question Sheila Rivenbark as soon as possible.

The employee parking area was empty, and the auditorium appeared to be deserted, but the door to the shop stood slightly ajar, so Cameron parked, and climbed up to the dock.

A wedge at the base of the door kept it from closing all the way, so he peered through the narrow opening. He said a tentative "hello" into the unlit workshop, but nobody answered. He cracked the door open a bit more to peer in, and saw someone hunched over a workbench, intently working on something under a dim lamp. Cameron opened the door wider to let in more light and said, "Mike?"

The person at the workbench whipped around, stole a quick glance at Cameron, and then bolted through the nearest stage door. The light had been too low for Cameron to recognize the person's face. Ordinarily, he would have let the matter ride, maybe to call Mike later and tell him what he observed. Under the current circumstances, he felt a need to identify the stranger, he headed through the door to the stage.

A set of dim safety lights on the back wall of the stage provided some illumination, but Cameron could see no one on stage and heard no footsteps. He stood stock-still, listening, and heard heavy breathing somewhere on the right side of the stage. As he tiptoed toward the sound, The breathing became less heavy, nearly imperceptible. He continued in the same direction until he came to the edge of a dressing-room door, where he caught a strong smell of stale cigarette smoke.

Cameron spoke in hushed tones, "Gus, it's Cameron Scott. We talked yesterday. Are you all right?"

No answer.

"Gus, I'm not here to hurt you or get you in troub—"

Someone slammed into Cameron so hard it knocked him face-first onto the stage floor. As his tackler ran by, Cameron caught an ankle and brought the person down. Cameron scrambled to his feet and prepared to defend himself, but the person stayed on the floor, unmoving. In a moment, a heavily breathing male voice said, "I swear, I was just trying to get some of my stuff that I left here when I quit."

Cameron, who was himself gasping for breath, only grunted, "I thought it was you. Get up."

Gus Danford scrambled to his feet, but made no attempt to get away. He said, "Please don't call the cops."

Cameron said, "How did you get in?"

"I had an extra master key made when I worked here. I swear, I only want my stuff back. I'm sure Mike already told everybody not to let me back in, so I had to do it this way."

"What stuff did you leave?"

"Some electronics equipment. I loaned it to Mike when they were having trouble with the house sound system. Come on, man, let me get it and I'll never come back here again."

"I can't let you take anything out of here, Gus. If it turned out not to be yours, I'd be an accessory to burglary. Your best bet is to go get back in your car and head home. Speaking of which, where is your car? I didn't see it anywhere when I came in."

"I parked it on the other side of campus and walked over here."

"If you want, I'll give you ride to your car, but you need to leave.

Now."

Danford hesitated. He tensed and started rocking back and forth. Cameron braced for a fight, but Danford finally relaxed and said, "All right, I'll go. Maybe I'll call Billy Twyford tomorrow and see if he'll get my stuff for me."

"Good idea. Do you need that ride?"

"Nah. I'm good, thanks."

Cameron pointed toward the workshop. "Okay, let's go." He escorted Danford out the door and pulled it shut, then watched him walk around the corner of the building, presumably toward his car. After Danford disappeared, Cameron got into his truck and cruised slowly out the driveway, hoping to see where he had parked. He finally caught sight of him about a hundred yards away, near a small cluster of cars in the main campus parking lot. Cameron stopped and watched as Danford looked warily around him, climbed into a beat-up old Ford, and drove off. Cameron did not see anyone else walking in the parking lot, but within several seconds after Danford left, a van eased out of a parking space and drove away.

By the time Cameron made his way from the driveway to the main parking lot, and then to the main highway, no cars were in sight. He gave up the chase and went home.

On the drive home, a thought entered Cameron's mind: *"I wonder why Gus didn't set off an alarm when he went in. Surely somebody would have changed the security code after he quit."*

Cameron phoned Ben. He told Ben about his encounter with Danford and said, "Okay, Mr. Criminal Lawyer, what are the chances I'll get busted for breaking into the building, or for letting Danford go?"

Ben pondered for a moment and said, "I'm not sure I'd call it a B&E, but you might want to let the sheriff know about the intruder as soon as you can."

"Good idea. He hasn't heard from me in a little while."

"You mean he hasn't had the gut-wrenching feeling of 'What's he getting me into now,' don't you?"

Cameron laughed. "Probably. All right, talk to you later."

Next, Cameron gave Elliott a ring. He filled Elliott in on the details of his chance meet-up with Gus, and added, "Looks like Mike Stevens might want to get the locks changed right away, wouldn't you agree?"

"I sure would agree. I need to talk with him about security measures for the Governor's visit anyway. Do you want us to pick Danford up for assault?"

"Nah. It would be his word against mine at this point. Besides, I guess I technically trespassed as much as he did, so you'd have to take us both in. I'd sure keep him under tight scrutiny though."

"Oh yeah, he's on my radar now. Listen, I'll let you know when Mr. Stevens and I can get together, and if you can sit in on the conversation, that would be great."

"Okay, keep me posted."

"Bring Ken along, too, if he can make it."

"I'll let him know."

When the call ended, Cameron called Ben back and said, "Looks like you'll need to be in 'fill in for Cameron' mode the next few days."

Ben said, "Gotcha. Like I've said, I'd rather do that than get mixed up in your crazy messes."

Shortly, Ken called and asked, "anything new on our agenda today?"

Cameron filled him in on the confrontation with Gus and his phone conversation with Elliott, and said, "If you don't mind, I need you to keep your calendar flexible for the next few days. Elliott wants us to meet with him and Mike Stevens about auditorium security."

Ken said, "Works for me." Referring to Cameron's ever-present pocket calendar, he added, "Don't forget to update your antique event-tracking device."

"Okay, smart-ass, I'll do that. At least I don't have to worry about my device getting a dead battery." His phone buzzed and he told Ken, "Gotta get this, it's Elliott.

Cameron answered his phone with, "Got hold of Mike already?"

Elliott said, "Actually, he got hold of me. Right after I hung up with you, dispatch let me know he'd called with some concerns. I'm going to call him back right now, and I'll let you know what I find out."

"Okay, thanks."

Shortly, Elliott called to tell Cameron that Stevens's best time to talk about security measures would be Sunday at two. Cameron told Elliott that he and Ken would be there, and texted the information to Ken when he pulled into his driveway.

♪

Mary had lunch ready when Cameron got home. As soon as he walked in the door, her eyes widened, and she said, "Who the hell'd you tick off this time?"

Cameron said, "What do you mean?" She reached out and lightly touched his forehead and he said, "Ouch. What in the world?"

"Go look in the mirror."

Cameron went to the nearest bathroom mirror to look, saw the black and blue knot on his forehead, and came back to the kitchen, saying, "You should have seen what I did to the other guy." He laughed, and Mary sort-of smiled in return, saying "But really. What happened?"

Cameron caught Mary up on the morning's events, and Mary said, "Do you need to get that looked into? Looks pretty nasty."

"It doesn't feel as bad as it looks, but if it gets worse overnight, I'll call our doctor tomorrow, okay?"

"All right. I don't need you passing out from a concussion."

"Speaking of tomorrow, I've got to meet with Elliott over at the auditorium at two. We're supposed to talk with the manager about security for the Governor's visit."

Mary said, "Be sure to let Elliott know about Mr. Danford's extra key. What do you think they'll do about that."

"I already told him about the key, but you know what? In all the confusion, I forgot to make Gus give it to me. Most likely, they'll change the lock anyway, so no problem. I imagine they'll make new keys and restrict them to certain personnel."

"I wonder why they haven't gone to a keyless system?"

"Good question. Budget? Somebody didn't see at as necessary? If somebody doesn't bring it up tomorrow, I will, along with a question about the lack of alarms. Meanwhile, let's eat."

CHAPTER FOURTEEN

At two o'clock Sunday afternoon, Mike Stevens stood waiting at the front lobby door of the auditorium to greet the security detail. He conducted Elliott, Cameron, Ken, and Elliott's chief deputy, Paul Amatio, to his office and offered them seating on the couch and chairs in front of his desk, then settled into his chair. Cameron had a fleeting thought about the 'casting' couch before he sat.

Elliott opened the conversation. "As you know, Mr. Stevens, we're here to talk about the concert on Thursday, when Governor Danford will be here to see his niece in the band. I guess the first thing to bring up is the run-in that Mr. Scott had with the Governor's nephew Gus Danford, yesterday afternoon."

Stevens said, "I was shocked to hear about it." To Cameron, he added, "I'm not sure why you came when you did, but I'm glad you found out about Gus's extra key." He pointed to Cameron's head. "Is that a souvenir of yesterday's confrontation?"

Cameron said, "I'm afraid so. I'm not sure Gus meant to hurt me; he tried to run past me but slammed into me in the dark. I grabbed him by the ankle to stop him, so he might be walking with a little bit of a limp today."

Stevens said, "I'm awfully sorry. I hope that heals fast."

"It'll be fine. Let me ask you though; isn't there some sort of alarm for that door?"

A touch of crimson rose in Stevens's neck. "We have one, but I had to disable it because it started going off for no reason. I didn't want it to blast out in the middle of a performance. I've been trying to get the company that installed it to come out and fix it, but they keep putting me off."

Elliott said, "Willis Security Systems?"

Stevens said, "Yes, as a matter of fact. How did you know that?"

"State Bureau of Investigation looked into it for me. Willis is usually pretty good about following up on calls. Let me give them a call and light a fire under them."

As he started pulling up the Willis number on his phone, Elliott asked Stevens, "Have you thought about installing a keyless entry on the back door? I see there's one on the lobby doors."

"Unfortunately, our budget's been too tight this year. We had to stay shut down for so long during the pandemic that our revenues fell far short of projections. In fact, the school's been absorbing a lot of our ongoing costs, and repaying them to the general fund out of our budget a little at a time."

By the time Stevens finished speaking, Elliott had connected with the security company. He said, "Chris? Hey, Sheriff Grainger here. Listen, I've been going over some security concerns with Mike Stevens at the auditorium, and he says he's been trying to get you to fix his back-door alarm system for a while now. We need to get that done by tomorrow. Think you can handle it? Oh, and he really needs a keyless entry system for that door, but says the school hasn't budgeted one yet."

Elliott listened for a while, interjecting an 'uh-huh' or 'I see' from time to time, and then said, "I appreciate it. I'll let Mr. Stevens know to let you in tomorrow after one-thirty. Thanks, Chris."

Elliott smiled as he ended the call. "Got that cleared up. You'll need to be here at tomorrow in time to let Chris Willis and his crew in. They're going to fix the alarms and install a new keyless door lock, and hold the billing for next budget cycle. I don't know if I've mentioned it, but his company's been a big donor to the Governor's campaign in the past."

Stevens, looking a bit bewildered, stammered, "Oh, uh, yes, certainly, I'll be here. Thank you so much."

Elliott said, "Let's get on to some other things. Since our sniffer dog alerted to explosives residue in that cymbal case, I'll have a K-9 officer here early on Thursday, and we want the dog to sniff everything–and everybody–that comes in here."

"That might cause a little backup for people coming in, but it should be doable."

"Okay, we'll need to bring the Governor and whoever's with him through a separate entrance–maybe the workshop entry door?"

"We have a side door that leads to a small vestibule and then straight into the seating area. That might work better."

"Perfect. You can show us that one when we tour the building in a bit. Mr. Scott, any questions before we start looking around?"

Cameron said, "I hate to keep harping on that stage brick incident, but I still worry about how it happened and what's being done to keep something like that happening ag–"

Stevens held up a hand. "I, uh, I think I can clear that up for you right now. I'm at fault."

Cameron and everyone else stared in stunned silence.

Stevens continued, "I'm awfully embarrassed to admit this, and ashamed of how I acted, but I'm the one who accidently knocked that brick off the rail."

Cameron looked at Stevens doubtfully, to which he replied, "I know what I told you, but when it happened, but I was actually on the flyrail, trying to figure out why our main curtain's been binding lately. One of the stagehands told me that the weight ratios checked out okay, but it's been hard to bring it in and out. Anyway, while I fiddled with the curtain rope, I accidently bumped into the stack of bricks and knocked off the top one. When I saw how close I came to causing major damage to someone, I...well, I lost it. I didn't see anybody looking upward, so I quietly hightailed it to the circular staircase, snuck across the grid to an exit on the other side, and went back to my office the back way."

Cameron said, "And you've let us worry and waste our time looking for the culprit?"

Elliott laid a hand on Cameron's arm and said, "I'm glad you've eliminated that worry for all of us. I do expect you to let the concert band folks know what really happened, and work it out with them from there."

Ken added, "If you haven't already done it, I'd suggest you find a better system for stacking the stage bricks."

Stevens nodded sheepishly. "I've already had our stagehands rearrange them so they're all below the top of the steel apron. I should have done that long ago, but I guess it was one of those things that just...happens. Everybody gets wrapped up in changing out the weights and isn't as careful as they should be about where they place them. I guess it sounds like I'm trying to shift the blame, but I do know that it's ultimately my responsibility to keep up with that sort of thing."

Elliott said, "I suppose that's between you and whoever your boss is."

"That would be the college president. I'll give him an incident report and face any disciplinary action he might want to take. This whole thing's been weighing heavily on my conscience."

Elliott said, "Well, like I said, I'm glad to have that concern eliminated." Cameron said nothing.

The group turned their attention to the task at hand and Stevens led them on a tour of the facility, including an event center connected to the auditorium, with a 'basement' mechanical room under it, the over-stage grid and its entrances, the front-of-house lighting rail over the audience, and what Stevens called a 'trap room', which turned out to be under-stage storage space.

The end of the tour took them back to the lobby door, where

Elliott said, "All right, Mr. Stevens, thank you very much for the tour, and we'll be letting you know our security plan after we have a chance to meet and hash things out."

On the way to the parking lot, Elliott asked Cameron, "You didn't look like you were entirely satisfied with Mike's explanation about the falling steel weight."

Cameron took a few seconds to answer. "No, not entirely. I can't exactly put my finger on it, but something didn't ring true about the whole thing." He turned to Ken and said, "What did you think?"

Ken nodded. "I agree. I guess Cameron and I are going to have to talk it over. I wanted to believe him, but something in the back of my mind put up a red flag."

Elliott said, "Let me know if you figure it out. In the meantime, let me tell you what Chris Willis said about the alarm and the door lock. According to him, nobody ever called him about either one."

Cameron said, "Really? Why didn't you mention that to Stevens?"

"We had too much else to worry about for today. Well, if you think of what's bothering you about Mike's mea culpa, let me know. In the meantime, Detective Amatio and I are gonna work out a security plan and we'll have to discuss with the Governor's security detail. We've worked general security over here before, but nothing to extent we'll be facing on Thursday."

They all said their good-byes and climbed into their cars. Ken and Cameron had come together in Cameron's truck, and on the way back, Cameron said, "Why do both of us have alarms jangling in the back of our heads over Mike's surprise confession?"

"I dunno. Maybe the way he didn't look anybody in the eye. Maybe the way it seemed too rehearsed. I really don't know."

"Same here. One thing I do remember from our first trip up to the flyrail though; I didn't see any brick piles anywhere near that main curtain rope. At least when we were up there, they were all piled further away."

"Good point. Somebody checking the main curtain couldn't have knocked one of those bricks off. The brick that dented the stage had to have been at least ten feet down the rail from the main. You know what? Now that I think about it–the lock for the main is located at stage level, not up at the flyrail. He couldn't have been checking it from up there."

Both of them grew quiet for a bit, then Cameron spoke. "Okay, next question: Who's Mike covering for, and why's he willing to take the fall? I mean, if the college administration felt like lives were endangered, that could have cost him his job."

Ken said, "True. I'd think that'd be a major offense. If nothing else they'd be worried about the costs if somebody got seriously hurt or killed."

"Yeah, monetary and publicity costs. You know–something just dawned on me. If Gus had a spare key to the workshop, it could easily have been him up on the flyrail. I don't know why he'd have been there, or why Stevens would cover for him if he knew, but it's something else to think about."

"Yet another complication."

Cameron laughed. "I know. We don't have enough to worry about already. By the way, I still haven't had a chance to talk with the lighting director, Ms.–shoot–what's her name?"

"Sheila Rivenbark. You know, I think there's a way you can get her to come into the office, but it'll take a few calls."

Cameron lifted a brow. "Really? Wanna clue me in?"

"Umm...let me make my calls and see if they pan out, okay?"

"No problem. If it gets her in to talk with us, that's great."

Cameron dropped Ken off at his house, and drove home to spend the rest of the day working on the yard with Mary.

CHAPTER FIFTEEN

On Monday morning, Ken met Cameron at the office door with the news, "Ms. Rivenbark can be here at two o'clock this afternoon. Hope you're available."

"Great. Come on with me and I'll check my calendar. If there's anything on it, I'll rearrange. Meanwhile, you can tell me your secret to digging her up."

"It's not going to sound like much when I tell it, but I finally remembered to have Mia call her and mention a few things, and here we are."

"I look forward to meeting her." Cameron flipped through his calendar. "Looks like I'm clear at two. Let's meet with her in your office. See you then."

Cameron busied himself with office work, took an early lunch, and plowed back into some more work until his phone buzzed at two. Ken let him know that he was on his way to the lobby to meet with Sheila, and would take her back to his office.

The first words out of Sheila's mouth when Cameron walked into Ken's office were, "Is it true what I've heard about you?"

Cameron smiled, shook her hand, and said, "Let's get settled in, and let me hear what you've heard about me before I answer that."

When everyone got seated, Cameron said, "Now, tell me what you've heard about me."

"Mia told me about all kinds of things, like helping to save the President's life, and doing battle with drug dealers and stuff."

Cameron shifted a glance toward Ken, who shifted in his seat uncomfortably. He drew in a long breath and exhaled slowly. "I've helped some clients out of situations that posed a little danger, yes. But you understand, I don't talk about it much because of client confidences, as, ahem, Ken can tell you."

By the crimson rising above Ken's collar, Cameron could tell that the 'few things' Mia told Sheila had come from him.

Cameron continued, "Ken tells me that you and his lady friend Mia know each other through a German-American club, but you don't sound very German to me."

Sheila said, "I was born in Germany, and my parents are German, but I've been in the U.S. for a long time. I thought it'd be a good idea to join the club to keep up with my fading German language skills."

"I'm surprised we didn't see you at the recent Oktoberfest."

"Believe me, I wanted to go, but we had a show that day and I had to work. That's the way it is with backstage work–lots of missed weekends."

"Understood. I guess Mia gave you some idea of why we wanted to see you?"

"Something about things going on backstage, I think? I don't know if I can help you much. I usually keep to myself except to talk about lighting issues."

Ken said, "I didn't give Mia much detail."

Cameron said, "As you probably know, the Governor's going to come to the concert on Thursday night, because his niece is in the band. I guess you also know about the stage brick that nearly hit one of the band's players at a rehearsal."

"Well, of course, all of us know about Danford's visit. Mr. Stevens hasn't shut up about it. He's about as giddy as a damn school girl. But as far as the stage brick incident, I don't know anything about it. I didn't need to be at work until after it happened that day, so I don't have much detail."

"Were you aware that Mr. Stevens 'fessed up to knocking the brick off the rail?"

"No. He said we were going to have a special meeting tonight, but he didn't mention his confession. How did you find out?"

"He told us. Us being the Sheriff, Ken and me."

"I can't believe that Mr. Perfect would own up to making a mistake."

"Really?"

"As far as he's concerned, we all make mistakes that he has to fix. Did he say how it happened?"

"That's one of the things we wanted to ask you about. According to him, when he was on the flyrail trying to find out why the main curtain kept binding, he accidently kicked a brick off a nearby stack."

"Makes sense."

"Makes sense until you think about two things. One, the rope brake for the main is at stage level; and two, there were no bricks stacked close enough to the main's rope for him to have 'accidently' kicked one off."

Cameron looked intently into Sheila's eyes to see her reaction. Her pupils dilated considerably at first, and then she quickly averted her gaze floorward. It took her several seconds to respond. "I, uh,..."

Cameron said, "Ken and I think that Mr. Stevens is covering for someone, but we can't understand why. Do you have any ideas about that?"

Sheila stumbled a bit again, and then lifted her gaze straight toward Cameron. "I guess I should have known better to come talk to a lawyer. Is this some kind of cross-examination?"

"No. We're not out to 'get' you. We're simply trying to find out what kind of dangers that auditorium holds. I can tell that you know something, and it would be better to tell us here and now rather than after an arraignment."

Cameron could see a bit of tremor in Sheila's hands, and her straighforward gaze faltered. With a low, shaking voice, she said, "I think he's covering for Gus Danford. You know who he is?"

"Your former box office manager, yes. How do you figure that?" Cameron did not mention his former meetup with Gus.

"Mike and Gus were always tight. Gus quit because he couldn't take a little ribbing. You know how people start ragging each other in the workplace, but nobody means it."

"I understand that you gave him some of that ribbing. Something to do with his possible relationship to the Governor?"

"No big deal. I'd rag on what a crappy job Danford was doing and he'd get pissed and storm off."

"He never gave any of it back to you?"

"Nah. I think he knew I was right, and that's what pissed him off."

"And you thought it was a good idea to bring up supercharged politics in the work place?"

"I wouldn't call it that. Just friendly banter's all. But I didn't know he'd be such a pansy about it."

"And Mr. Stevens never intervened?"

"I think Gus bitched to him, but I guess Mike saw it the same way I did, because he never said anything to me."

Cameron sat back quietly in his chair, absorbing Sheila's revelations. He looked toward Ken, to see if he had any questions.

Ken said, "Ms Rivenbark, do you get up on the lift to adjust stage lights, or does your TD do that?"

"That's the TD's job. My job's to run the console."

"So, you don't go up into the FOH lighting rail either?"

"No. Like I said, that's Trail Boss's job. At least at our place it is. He kind of rules the roost as far as that stuff goes. Of course, since we've been replacing the old stage lights with LED lighting the last couple of years, a lot of the adjustment gets done from the console now, or an ipod."

"But there's still some of the old lighting left?"

"Trail Boss and Mr. Stevens have been working to get all of it replaced, as the budget will allow, but yeah, there's still a few 'antiques' left, especially at FOH." Sheila snorted a laugh.

"Okay, it's pretty obvious that you and Mr. Danford didn't get along. How about the rest of the crew. Any problem with any of them?"

"I don't have that much contact with many of the stagehands 'n'em. I have my stuff to do and they have theirs, y'know?"

"So, no problems then?"

"Nah."

"No 'banter' between you and them?"

"Um, well, I mean once in a while, but like I said, we don't cross each others' paths that much. Most of us are part-timers, so we only see each other once in a while."

"Okay. That's all I've got. Cameron?"

Cameron said, "I understand you worked with Governor Danford's campaign last election. Is that right?"

"Yeah, that sorry son of a ...well anyway, I expected him to hire me full time after the election, but that didn't happen."

"Did he promise you that he'd hire you?"

"Not directly. I didn't get the much chance to talk to him personally, but the campaign manager kept telling me what a great job I did and all, so I assumed..."

"I see. Do you hold that against Governor Danford?"

"Oh hell no. I hold it against the manager is all. I mean, Danford does what his people tell him, you know? He's not really that bright."

"Do you know whether Mr. Stevens holds any rancor toward the Governor?"

"Mike? Psh, best I can tell, he thinks Danford's a saint. I guess that's why he's so excited about him coming to the auditorium."

Cameron stood and said, "All right, well, thank you for coming by, Ms. Rivenbark. Mr. Benton will see you out." He gave a 'come back here' look to Ken as they walked out.

Ken came back to his office to talk with Cameron about the interview. Cameron said, "What did you think about Ms. Rivenbark?"

"She seems to be quite taken with herself, for one. And fine with attacking a co-worker over politics. I'm not sure why Mike puts up with that."

"I gathered from talking with Jodie that he dallies with his female staff rather freely, so she might be another of his dalliances. I mean, she's not bad looking, in a rough kind of way."

"True. Good point about why he'd cover for her."

"So where now?"

"Now, we try to get one step ahead of whoever might be planning to harm Governor Danford, if such a person exists. We've only got 'til Thursday to figure it out, so let's–"

Ken's office phone buzzed. He picked it up. "What's up, Nedra? Really? Cameron's here with me, so I'll let him know. Thanks." He hung up and told Cameron, "Looks like we've got one less suspect."

Cameron shot an eyebrow up. "Really? Who?"

"Gus Danford. Nedra just heard it, or rather read it. Local social media's abuzz." Ken reached for his computer keyboard. "Yup, here's something: 'Nephew of Governor Danford found dead of apparent suicide on local beach.' I'll send you a link." He tapped a few keys and then went back to reading. "Looks like it happened about eleven this morning. Some beach runners found him in a quiet part of the island, halfway buried in sand."

"Does it say what means he used to commit the suicide?"

"Let's see.... Ah, here. Looks like he overdosed on something. He's been sent to the morgue and they're going to get labs done. Who knows how long that'll take."

"Considering his connection to the Governor, it might be expedited."

"True." Ken scanned the screen a little more and then said, "Looks like that's about it for now."

"Opening a whole new line of thought. One: Are we really

looking at suicide? And Two: If not, who's responsible and why? Let me see what Elliott might know." Cameron punched in Elliott's speed dial button and put the phone on speaker mode.

Elliott answered, "Gus Danford, found this morning. No labs yet. Right?"

"Man, what a mind reader. I know the story so far is suicide, but after my run-in with him, I'm thinking not. Think this'll change the Governor's mind about coming?"

"I doubt it, although we're expecting word from his office any time now. So, why do you think it's not suicide?"

"I know he's been down on his luck lately, but he seemed like too much of a survivor to me. Can't put my finger on it, and I'm certainly no psychologist, but he didn't seem like the suicidal type."

"Well, a lot of people can mask depression pretty well, so don't count it out."

"True. I guess the lab results will tell us something."

"You probably guessed that there's a priority on getting them back. So we should know within a couple of days."

"Okay. Keep us posted. Meanwhile, Ken and I will keep brainstorming. I'm still obsessed about that hunk of steel falling from the flyrail because I think there's a connection. But then again, I could be dead wrong."

"Don't get too hung up on it. There's still plenty of other stuff to worry about. Catch you later."

"Okay. Bye."

Cameron said to Ken, "Got any thoughts?"

Ken said, "Let's hash out the idea of Gus having something to do with the brick falling. Why would he have been up there? And where would he have gone to hide after it happened?"

"Looks like the 'where would he have gone to hide' part is pretty easy. My guess is that he would have taken the same route that Mike says he took."

"That would be my guess, too. But why in the world would he

have kicked or thrown the brick down in the first place? Did he somehow want to get even with Mike? Did he hate somebody in the band that mu–"

Cameron said, "What? You think he really did target somebody in the band? The tuba player? Or somebody else."

"Somebody else. Didn't we learn that Danford's niece plays clarinet in the band?"

"Whoa, that's right. I wonder how close her connection is to Gus. All we know is that he's supposed to be the governor's nephew, but we don't know if he's the niece's brother or her cousin. And we don't know if any animosity runs between them."

"Who knows what kind of secrets stay hidden within families?"

"It's worth looking into. I wonder if there's a chance we could talk to...did we ever learn her first name?"

"No. All we know is that she's Danford's niece. In fact, we don't even know if Danford is her last name."

"Good point. Looks like another call to Jeff is in order. You want to handle it?"

"Sure. Let's hope he's available." Ken took out his phone and speed-dialed Jeff. He got Jeff's 'not in' notice and said, "Hey, Jeff, this is Ken Benton again. I need another favor if you can call me back as soon as you can."

Ken ended the call and said, "I'm sure he's at work, but I hope he can break free soon to call back."

Cameron said, "In the meantime, we can get some office work done, so let me know if you find anything out."

Two hours passed before Ken buzzed Cameron, saying, "According to Jeff, our clarinet playing niece is Katrina Knowles. He looked up her number on the band roster for me. Want me to come to your office for us to call her?"

"Tell you what; how 'bout you give her a call and find when she can come on in here. We'll arrange our schedules for whenever that may be."

"Okay. I'll let you know."

Some time after four, Ken again buzzed Cameron with an update. "She won't be able to see us until after she gets off work at five-thirty. She said six o'clock would allow time for her to wrap up at work and get over here."

"Okay, great. I'll let Mary know I'll be a little late and we'll keep ourselves busy until then."

Cameron immediately called Mary's work number and left a message and then retired to the office library for some research on a real estate issue he had been working on. He had left word for the staff to leave the front door unlocked when they left at five. He also asked secretary Penny if she would stay late to 'chaperone' while he and Ken interviewed a young lady.

CHAPTER SIXTEEN

At six, Cameron heard the front door open, and Penny saying, "You must be Mr Scott's six o'clock appointment. I'll let him know you're here." He left his research work on the table and strolled to the front, meeting up with Ken, on the way. They introduced themselves to Ms. Knowles, an attractive young lady with waist-length auburn hair who reminded Cameron of Mary in her college years, and escorted her to Cameron's office.

When everyone got settled, Cameron said, "I'm sure you're wondering why we wanted to talk with you."

Katrina said, "Jeff Kelly texted me and gave me a heads up. Something to do with my uncle coming to the concert? Is somebody suing somebody over it or something?"

Cameron chuckled. "I guess it does seem a little odd that lawyers want to talk to you about that. No, we're actually helping the sheriff's office with security. I won't bore you with the details of how we're involved with that, but we would like to ask you a few questions about recent events at Graves Auditorium. First, though, we'd like to offer our condolences for the loss of your cousin, Gus, assuming he was your cousin."

"He was. Thank you. We weren't that close, but it was still a shock."

"Were you and he at odds for some reason?"

"No. Nothing like that. My mother and Uncle Phil have always been very close..."

"Uncle Phil is Governor Danford?"

Yes. But Gus's father, Uncle Oren, has always been the black sheep of the family, and we all thought Gus would be exactly like him. In fact, I think Gus only moved down here to try and take advantage of my mother. She's very sweet and generous, and he gave her a hard-luck story about how people kept working against him and all that. She tried to help him out–even let him live at her place for a while, but Dad put a stop to that when things started to go missing around the house. Dad swore that Gus stole them, so he kicked him out."

"I think you know about the metal stage brick that almost hit your band's tuba player. Were you anywhere near Mr. Westheimer when that happened?"

Katrina stared wide-eyed back and forth between Ken and Cameron. "You think somebody tried to hit me with that thing? I don't really think so. I mean, that would have been terrible aim, with me clear across the stage with the rest of the clarinet section."

"I'm glad to hear you weren't in danger. Did you happen to look up toward the fly-rail when it happened?"

"Good heavens no. All of us looked at where the sound came from, at stage-level. I don't think anybody thought to look upward. Except...wait a minute. My friend Dolores did say something like, 'Wonder what he's doing up there?' right after we heard the big crash. Most of us clarinetists were standing where the wing curtains blocked part of the view, but from where she stood, she could see between the curtains."

Ken said, "Could you give us Dolores's last name? And do you know how to get hold of her?"

Katrina took out her cell phone, punched a few buttons and said, "Here you go."

Ken wrote down the name 'Dolores Taylor' as well as the phone number that appeared by her name, and said, "That's very helpful, thanks."

Cameron said, "I hate to ask you this, but do you have any idea why someone would want to kill Gus?"

Katrina hesitated. "Kill him? I thought they said he committed suicide. Why do you think somebody killed him?"

"Just a hunch. You probably know him better than I do, but he seemed like too much of a survivor to me to be the type who would do himself in."

Ken chimed in, "Cameron and I both had the same impression of him."

Katrina pondered for a moment. "You know, you might be right. During the time he lived with mom, he always talked about big plans for the future. Even when things went terribly wrong for him, he still always looked to the future. I wouldn't have called him a joyful sort, but I never saw him get really down either. Don't get me wrong–he still took after his dad in a lot of ways, but I certainly wouldn't call him a quitter."

Cameron said, "So, you wouldn't say he had any reason to want to harm you? Or your uncle?"

"Oh heavens no. On the contrary. He always defended Uncle Phil. Said he wished Uncle Phil had been his father."

Cameron looked toward Ken. "Anything else?"

Ken shook his head 'no' and said, "All right, Ms. Knowles, we thank you for coming by. Rest assured that everything possible is being done to assure your uncle's safety, and the information you've given us has been very helpful."

Katrina did not appear to be terribly assured as she shook their hands and left. As soon as she left, Cameron went to the front to thank Penny, and told her she could take a couple of hours off to make up for it. He went back to the office and told Ken, "Let's call Ms. Taylor right now."

Ken tapped the numbers into his cell phone, and after a few

rings, someone answered. "Hello? I think you might have a wrong number. I don't know any lawyers."

"Please don't hang up. Katrina Knowles gave us your number and said you might know something about the accident at Graves Auditorium the other week. We're trying to find out how it happened." Ken put the phone on speaker mode and told Ms. Taylor, "I'm here with attorney Cameron Scott, and I'm putting you on speakerphone so Mr. Scott can hear you as well."

"You're talkin' about the chunk of metal that almost killed Mr. Westheimer? I don't think there's anything I can tell you about that."

"Ms. Knowles said you saw somebody at the rail right after it happened."

"Oh, that. I saw somethin' movin' overhead and looked up is all."

"Did you see somebody you recognized?"

"I couldn't swear to it, 'cause they moved out of the way fast, but first thing I thought was, 'That's Mr. Hall'."

"Mr. Hall?"

"Yeah, George Hall, the technical director at the auditorium. Hard to miss that flamin' red hair. But like I said, I saw him for, like, half a second and he disappeared, so I could have imagined it."

"Do you remember which direction he went?"

"Um, I think upstage. You know, toward the back of the stage? But like I said, I only saw him for a second, and then the curtains blocked the view."

"Okay, thank you Ms. Taylor. You've been very helpful."

"Helpful for what?"

"We've been investigating how that 'chunk of metal' fell in the first place, and you've given us some important information."

"Are you suing the auditorium?"

"No. Nobody's hired us to do that. We're actually helping with security for the governor's upcoming visit."

"Oh yeah. Kats...um...Katherine, told me about that. In fact, I think she's the one that invited him to come. Well, she invited him after Loretta told her how cool it would be. Kats usually doesn't make a big deal about him being her uncle and all, but she's pretty excited that he wants to come down here. I guess about every politician in the county's going to be there, too, so that gives us more audience."

"That doesn't make you nervous?"

"Pfsh. My mom's a county commissioner, and she comes to all the concerts, so it's no big deal to me to have a few more bigwigs."

"I could be mistaken, but you sound kind of young. How long have you been in the band?"

"I've only been in it about a year. I played in marching band in high school, and I'm a student at the community college now, so it's a good place to keep playing."

"I'm glad you have an outlet. Again, I want to thank you for helping out. If we think of any further questions, would you mind if we called you back?"

"Nah. Glad to help. Kats is a good friend, so I'm happy to see that you're helping her uncle."

Ken ended the call and said to Cameron, "I guess we've got a new lead to follow."

Cameron said, "And not much time to follow it. I'm not sure Mike'll be too excited about seeing me at the auditorium again, but I think I've got a way to guarantee he won't interfere if I swing by there." He pulled out his phone and hit a few buttons. Within a few rings, he said, "Elliott, can you do me a favor? Can you call the community college president and let him know that Ken and I are on your security team, so he can let Mr. Stevens at the auditorium know to cooperate with us? Great. We got a new lead on how the stage brick fell, and I want to follow up on that today. Yeah, it looks like the technical director might not have been too forthcoming about that. I think he might have been the cause for it, and Mike has covered up for it, although I don't know why. In fact, you might want to come out there with us this time. What's a good time for you? Great. See you there."

Cameron ended the call and told Ken, "Elliott says tomorrow morning at nineish is good for him." He next called Stevens. "Mr. Stevens? Cameron Scott here. I'd like you to meet with me and the sheriff at the auditorium tomorrow morning, let's say about nine? And make every effort to have your technical director, George Hall, there."

A long pause followed, and finally, Stevens answered, "I, I, I'll do my best to have him here. May I ask what this is about?"

"Sure. It's about why you wanted to take the blame for what your technical director did. We'll see you there." Before Stevens had a chance to answer, Cameron ended the call. He said to Ken, "Let's hope they both show up."

Ken said, "They should both be there anyway, as the only full-time employees."

"Good thought. I guess we'll see"

CHAPTER SEVENTEEN

At nine o'clock Tuesday morning, Cameron, Ken, and Elliott met at the auditorium workshop entrance, and briefly discussed strategy for the upcoming meeting before going in. Stevens met them at the door, looking the opposite of his usually dapper self. He had two days' worth of beard growth, his hair looked a mess, and his black backstage outfit looked like he'd slept in it. A short distance behind him stood George Hall, also clad in backstage black, but not as disheveled.

Immediately, Elliott said, "I'll have to ask both of you to clasp your hands behind your heads while I check for weapons." Both men's eyes widened, and Stevens asked shakily, "Are you here to arrest us?"

As he patted both of them down, Elliott said, "That depends on your answers to some questions we have." He finished the pat-down, stepped back, and nodded to Cameron.

Ken said, "I'd suggest we go to the green room to talk." He led them to a room near the stage, telling Cameron, "The 'green room' is where performers wait before they go on stage. Except for large groups who have to congregate in the shop or the event center at this auditorium."

They all went into the room and Elliott pointed out a couch, saying to Stevens and Hall, "Sit here." He then pulled three chairs in front of the couch, and he, Cameron and Ken sat in them. Pointing to Hall, he said, "I'll cut to the chase. We have a witness who saw you leaving the scene immediately after the steel weight fell from the flyrail. And yet you," pointing to Stevens, "took blame for the incident. We want the truth, and we want it now, about what happened and why. I don't need to tell you how important it is for us to know what's going on."

Stevens and Hall glanced back and forth at each other, and then Hall gave an almost imperceptible nod. Stevens said, "Honestly it was an accident. George is the one who bumped the brick and made it fall. Show him your ankle, George."

Hall pulled up his pant-leg and rolled down his sock to reveal a nasty bruise on his ankle. By this point, the bruise had mostly yellowed.

Stevens said, "Sheriff, you probably already know that Mr. Hall is on parole for an assault conviction in Rowan County."

Elliott said, "We do."

"Well, I'll tell you, he's the glue that holds things together around here. I'd be hard-put to find a replacement who could get things set up as expertly as he does. Now, think about it: A heavy weight almost hits somebody, a convicted felon's behind it. Don't you think people would automatically think he meant to do somebody harm?"

"I suppose so."

"I knew better, and took the risk of being fired rather than see him get arrested. Well, frankly, I knew it wouldn't be that much of a risk. I won't say I'm irreplaceable, but the school would be even harder-put trying to replace me in this job."

Cameron leaned forward and said, "We'll buy that excuse for the moment, but you'll need to explain why Mr. Hall had to be up there in the first place."

"To be blunt, we were looking for suspects."

"Suspects?"

"Yes, sir. Ever since we learned the Governor would be here for the concert, we've been hearing rumors that somebody in the band hated him and his policies so much that they were willing to do him harm."

Elliott said, "And you decided to play detective on your own and not warn us?"

Stevens said, "I know, I know, but at that point, all we had was a rumor to go on."

Elliott said, "I need names, right now. I don't care whether you think it's rumor."

Stevens and Hall again glanced back and forth at each other. Before they could answer, Cameron said, "Tell you what; I'm going to give you each a piece of paper, and I want you to write down the name or names of who you suspect." He tore two sheets of paper from a nearby tablet and handed one to each of them, saying, "Mike, you can use the end-table next to you to write on and George, you can use the counter-top over there by the coffee machine. Don't speak to each other."

Hall got up and moved to the counter and Stevens leaned over to the end-table to write. When each finished, Cameron said, "Hand your papers over to Sheriff Grainger. You can go ahead and sit back down, George."

Elliott took the papers from Hall and Stevens and Hall sat down. Ken, Elliott, and Cameron looked at the names they had written down: Both had written 'Jerry Dale and Loretta Jackson'. Elliott said, "Why would you suspect them?"

Stevens answered. "You remember that cymbal case that the sniffer dog zeroed in on?"

Cameron said, "The one nobody seemed to know about?"

"Yeah. One of our stage hands heard those two talking about it, and said that they said sounded like they knew more than they should."

Ken said, "Which stagehand?"

"Billy Twyford."

Ken, Cameron and Elliott all jotted down a note.

Elliott said to Hall, "From your position on the flyrail, could you see both of them?"

Hall said, "Not the whole time. They stood downstage talking for a while, and then Ms. Jackson ran upstage all of a sudden. When I turned to go where I could see her, my ankle caught the brick. I stayed long enough to make sure it didn't hurt anybody, and then hurried to see where Ms. Jackson went. That must have been when somebody saw me."

"And did you catch sight of Ms. Jackson again?"

"No. By that time, everybody'd rushed up to check on that tuba guy. I just wanted to get out of there, so I hightailed it up to the grid."

Elliott said. "It sounds plausible. For now. We're going to check out these two people, but in the meantime, not a word from either of you to anybody about this, understand?" He looked directly at Hall, "I don't need to tell you what effect interfering with an investigation could have on your parole, do I?"

Wide eyed, Hall said, "No sir."

Elliott continued, "Meanwhile, if you come across any further information, or if anything seems out of the ordinary while you set up for the concert, you let me or any of the security detail know immediately, understand?"

Hall and Stevens both nodded.

Elliott stood and said, "Thank you gentlemen. We'll be in touch." He led Ken and Cameron out of the building. Out in the parking lot, he said, "I'll run both names through the system. Meanwhile, see if you can find out where we can get hold of Mr. Dale and Ms. Jackson in a hurry. Cameron, good idea to have them write down the names separately, so they couldn't collude with each other over the answer."

Cameron said, "Thanks. Talk to you later."

Elliott left and Ken said, "I guess I'll get hold of Jeff one more time."

Cameron said, "Okay. I think I'll let Nedra know that we'll both be 'out of the office' through tomorrow. I get the feeling we'll be extremely busy."

Ken had already dialed his phone. "Jeff? Glad you answered. Look, I need some band member numbers, and I need you to keep what we're saying top-secret. Think you can do that? Good. I need numbers for..." he looked at the names he had jotted, "Loretta Jackson and Jerry Dale. Oh, and tell me what instruments they play." Ken wrote down what Jeff told him. "Okay, 'preciate it. I'll tell you what it's all about later." He ended the call and told Cameron the numbers and that Loretta played timpani and Jerry played auxiliary percussion.

Cameron said, "Hmm, auxiliary percussion would include things like crash cymbals, wouldn't it?"

"Sure would! We need to get that info to Elliott right now."

Cameron dialed Elliott's number and gave him the information they had gained from Jeff, and let him know that they would try to set up a meeting with the two percussionists as soon as they could. He also added, "They might be more willing to talk with Ken and me without somebody from law enforcement present, but that's your call."

Elliott paused for a bit. "I should be insulted, but I know what you mean. But be sure to keep me in the loop right away."

"Will do. Talk to you later."

Cameron said to Ken, "Why don't you call Loretta and I'll call Jerry.

They each dialed their respective percussionist and then talked over the results. Ken said, "Loretta didn't really want to talk to us, but I cajoled her into seeing us tomorrow morning at nine."

Cameron said, "Jerry didn't want to talk to us either, but he finally agreed to meet with us at his house tonight at eight. The address he gave me is a little ways out in the country, so why don't we meet at the office about seven-thirty and go from there."

"Okay, see you here this evening."

CHAPTER EIGHTEEN

At seven-thirty, Cameron and Ken met at the office to discuss their strategy for questioning Jerry Dale, and then drove out to his house. The house, a double-wide that had seen better days, sat on a small, well-kept lot, amid similar housing of varying shapes and sizes.

They parked at the curb and walked up a short concrete walkway to a rickety wooden platform that served as a front porch. To the left of the front door, a section of siding hung loose, although it appeared that someone had tried to tack it back up. A meowling tabby cat rubbed back and forth against Cameron's legs as he rang the doorbell. He peeked into the small door-window, seeing only eerie blue illumination that obscured details.

After a few minutes with no-one answering the bell, Cameron opened the storm door and rapped on the metal-clad main door. Right away, a ring of lights illuminated around the doorbell, and then a short flurry of footsteps sounded before the door opened. The man who opened it said, "I'm sorry–did you try to ring the doorbell? 'Cause if you did, it don't work. Guess I oughta put a sign on it, but I don't get much company anyways. I'm Jerry. C'mon in."

Jerry flipped a lightswitch on and stood aside for Cameron and Ken to enter. They filed into a smallish living room, crammed with a rump-sprung couch, some mostly-empty bookshelves, and an assemble-it-yourself desk. The couch faced a flat-screen television that covered a large portion of one wall. The desk occupied one corner of the room, its top littered with assorted piles of paperwork out of which rose a new-looking desktop computer–the source of the blue light. A rolling desk chair sat in front of the desk, turned toward them, with a pair of earphones still hanging over the back of it.

Jerry explained, "I had m'earphones on, playin'a video game, so I didn't hear you come up on the porch." After an awkward pause, he pointed toward the couch without looking at it and said, "Oh, um, please have a seat." They hesitated, looking at a mound of throw pillows, laundry, and old newspapers that completely covered the couch. He turned toward the couch and said, "Oh, wait," and sprinted over to throw it all on the floor. Cameron glimpsed at the newspapers on his way to the couch.

Once Ken and Cameron got seated, Jerry rolled the desk chair in front of them and plopped himself down into it. He said, "Can I get you something to drink? Coke, beer, or something?"

Cameron and Ken both shook their heads and said, "No, thanks."

Jerry said, "Oh, okay. So, what can I do for you?"

Cameron came right to the point. "I understand you're a percussionist with the concert band, and we'd like to ask you a few questions about recent events."

"Like, what kind of questions?"

"You probably heard about a stray cymbal case that showed up at the back of the auditorium stage."

Jerry fidgeted. "I don't know nothin' about that."

"Would you still say that if I told you that they found your fingerprints on the case?" Cameron knew that no fingerprints were found, but wanted to test Jerry's reaction.

Jerry had been looking floorward, but quickly shifted his gaze toward Cameron. "There should'na been any fingerprints on that case."

Cameron did not change his expression, but said, "I thought you didn't know nothin' about the case."

"Um, well, I mean, I kinda heard about it, but what I meant was that I didn't know how it got there. You know, I got a lot of stuff to do. I'm takin' classes at the community college and all, and I gotta do my homework, so..." He stood, expecting Ken and Cameron to stand as well, but they remained seated.

Cameron said, "We won't hold you up much longer. A couple more questions and we're done. One question: Were you raised here, in this county?"

"What? No. I grew up in Concord. Why?"

"I noticed that you had copies of the Cabarrus Citizen's Times on the couch."

Jerry looked back and forth from the newspapers to Cameron, then stomped over to the door. He opened it and said, "I really gotta ask you to leave. Now. I got a lot to do."

Cameron stood and said, "Okay, one last question, and then we're off to the sheriff's department. Can anybody account for your whereabouts around the time that the stage brick nearly hit your tuba player?"

"Yeah, the whole percussion section, okay?" Jerry pointed toward the door adamantly and said nothing more.

Cameron said, "Thanks for talking with us, Jerry. You've been very helpful." He and Ken walked out and Jerry slammed the door behind them.

Outside, Cameron said to Ken, "Okay, I'm gonna drive a couple of blocks and park. I want to go back and check on something in Jerry's side yard, and it's dark enough now to go back there."

"Aren't you afraid he'll see you?"

"Not me; us. It looked like he was engrossed in a computer game when we got there, and he'll probably go back to it. But, just in case, we'll stay in the shadows. It looks like he's got a ring camera on his doorbell, but he didn't know we were here until we knocked, so it might be a dummy or not working."

"How do we know he doesn't have other cameras?"

"I checked when we drove up, and I didn't see any."

"Okay, but let's be sure we don't do anything that'll get us both arrested. I don't think Ben'd be too excited about running the whole firm while we're both in jail."

"We'll do our best."

Cameron drove to a sparsely inhabited street a short distance away, and they walked from there back toward Jerry's house. About a block away from the house, Cameron said, "Let's cross the street; I don't think we'll trigger the camera from over there." They crossed and kept walking until they stopped at a large maple that had grown in the grass strip between the sidewalk and street, almost directly across from Jerry's house.

Cameron pointed to a low hedge dividing Jerry's yard from his neighbor's to the right. He whispered, "I'm going to trespass into that yard. I'll duck down and sneak behind that hedge until I can see into Jerry's back yard. Stay here and hide behind this tree, and if Jerry comes out of his house, buzz me." He took out his phone and set it on silent and fully dimmed and said, "Do the same with yours, okay?"

"Okay. Be careful."

When Cameron got to the edge of the hedgerow, he ducked down and scooted to a point where a nearby street light allowed him a good view of Jerry's back yard. He spotted what he'd hoped to see, and snapped a couple of pictures with his phone, first making sure the flash was off. Mid-task, his phone buzzed with a text from Ken, *"He's out front w/flashlight!"*

Cameron texted back, *"Stay put and wait."* He made a beeline across the neighbor's back yard, running as quietly as he could in the dark. Unfortunately, he did not see a small tricycle, tripped over it, and came down hard. His involuntary grunt, along with the 'thud' of his body slamming into the turf, pierced the stillness of the night.

Across the street, Ken heard Cameron's crash. Within a few seconds, Jerry bolted through his front door and looked around.

Cameron stood up, took a quick assessment of his physical state, found everything intact, and kept going until a chain-link fence blocked his path. He turned right and sprinted along the fence toward the front yard. He got halfway to the street when porch lights blinked on in the house beside him and a small dog started yapping from inside. He kept his head low until he got to the sidewalk, then ran across the street to join Ken.

Cameron puffed out, "Let's boogie," and they both took off and kept running until they reached Cameron's truck. Ken quickly regained his breath, but it took a while longer for Cameron's labored breathing to slow down. He handed his keys to Ken and said, "You drive–I'm feeling a little light-headed." Ken gave a worried glance at Cameron, but quickly jumped into the driver's seat.

Once underway, Ken asked, "Are you okay? There's not much light in here, but I can tell you look a little pale."

Cameron took a couple of deep breaths and said, "Yeah, I think I'm all right. I really gotta get some more exercise though, especially if I'm gonna keep doing this kind of thing."

"So, what in the world did you expect to find in Jerry's back yard? He must not have gone back to his computer game, 'cause he came out with a flashlight right after you crashed."

"Oh crap. Hope you could stay hidden."

"Yeah, the tree covered me enough. What the hell happened?"

"Soon as I got your text, I ran across the neighbor's back yard and 'found' a tricycle on the way. I think I banged up my shin, but I'm okay otherwise."

"I guess he couldn't figure out where the noise came from. He went flying back indoors and I guess toward the back. So, what did you find back there?"

"Jerry's van; an '05 Chevy."

"His van? What was so special about that?"

"Its front fender on the passenger side."

"Okay, what was so special about the fender?"

"It's white, and the rest of the van is red. Looks like maybe he hit a deer or something and that's the only fix he could afford. When we drove up to the house, I recognized the back of it sticking out from behind the house, but wanted to see the front of it."

"Okay, I got that, but what's his van got to do with anything?"

"Remember when I caught Gus Danford in the auditorium, and then watched to make sure he went straight to his car?"

"The day you got the bump on your noggin, yeah."

"Thanks for the reminder. At least I didn't hit my head this time. Anyway, right after Gus drove off, I saw that red van with the white fender pull out of the parking lot and follow him."

"So, you think Gus and Jerry were up to something together?"

"Can't say yet. I don't know if we've got enough information for a search warrant, but I'd bet that Jerry's place is a treasure trove of evidence. The fact that he's a percussionist, and had copies of the same newspaper that was found in that cymbal case might be enough."

"I'd say so."

"Oh, and there's something else I want to check on. I saw a note on his desk with the letters 'ONS' and the number '3/4' next to it. I think I know what it means, but I want to be sure."

Cameron took out his phone and called Elliott. He got 'leave a message' response and said, "This is Cameron, give me a call-back as soon as you can."

Ken raised an eyebrow. "Must be pretty busy if he's not answering your call."

"I imagine he's swamped with work right not, getting ready for Danford's visit. Hope he calls back soon. Meanwhile, let's go home."

"Sounds good to me."

Ken drove the truck back to the office, and before climbing into his own car, asked Cameron, "Are you sure you're okay? You still look pretty drawn out."

Cameron waved it off. "No, I'm fine. When we get done with all this, I'll make a doctor's appointment, but we've got too much to do right now. Listen, don't mention it to Mary; no sense getting her all upset over nothing. See you tomorrow. I'll let you know if I get hold of Elliott."

CHAPTER NINETEEN

When Cameron arrived at home, Mary said, "Any luck on the tuba caper?"

"The what?"

"You know–the brick thingie almost hitting the tuba player."

Cameron laughed. "Yes and no. Every time we think we're getting somewhere, a new wrinkle unfolds. Wait...wrinkles don't unfold, do they? I'll just say a new wrinkle develops."

This time, Mary laughed. "I think you've been working at this thing too hard. I didn't know when you'd be home, so I left a plate for you to nuke."

"Thanks. Think I'll heat it up and eat it at my desk. I've got a few things to sort out. Maybe you can help."

"Sure. There's nothing on television tonight anyway. Might as well entertain myself with your problems."

Cameron stood and stared at Mary for a moment. "You know, sometimes I can't tell if you're being serious or being sarcastic."

"Serious this time. I'll meet you in the office."

Cameron got his dinner warmed, went to the office and sat in his desk chair, plate in his lap. Mary came in and sat in a chair facing him.

Cameron said "I put a call in to Elliott a little while ago, but he hasn't called back yet, so we might get interrupted, but here's what transpired today." He nibbled on his dinner while went over what had happened at Jerry Dale's house—leaving out the part where he nearly passed out—and then added, "Maybe you can help me with a little puzzle. I saw a slip of paper on his desk that said, 'ONS 3/4.' I've been trying to figure out if that's got anything to do with the 'tuba caper'.

Mary cocked her head for a moment and then her eyes brightened. "ONS; Old North State. And I remember the song being in three-quarter time when we listened to it"

Cameron slapped himself in the forehead. "Well, duh. I'd say it does have something to do with the tuba caper, big time." As soon as he got done speaking, his phone rang. He answered with, "Hey Elliott, I've got some important information, and Mary helped me decipher what could be a key element." After a short pause he said, "What? Oh, don't worry about it—I know you've got a ton of things to do right now. Listen, I think you might want to get a warrant to search Jerry Dale's house asap." He related the afternoon's events to Elliott, adding, "I've got a hunch that The Old North State song figures into whatever plans are hatching. Don't you think this new information will convince Danford to skip the concert?" He listened to Elliott's response and said, "All right, well...let me know if you get that warrant. Thanks. Talk to you later."

After Cameron ended the call, Mary said, "I can't tell if you're puzzled or pissed, but your eyes are telling me something."

Cameron first responded with a short shake of the head and then said, "Elliott kind of acted like I was bothering him. I dunno...maybe there's been a lot going on behind the scenes that I don't know about, so I shouldn't read too much into it, but I got the feeling that he's not going to get that warrant."

"What? Are you kidding?"

"He thanked me for the information, but said he had everything under control, said 'Bye' and hung up."

"Well, if he says it's under control, maybe you should take his word for it."

"I suppose you're right. But I still get a nagging feeling that something's not quite right."

"One of your hunches?"

"Yeah, that's a good way to put it."

"You've had a pretty good track record with those hunches, so why don't you take some quiet time to mull it over. I've got plenty of things I can do." She started to get up, but Cameron said, "No, stick around, if you don't mind. You can help me sort this out."

She eased back into her chair, saying, "Exactly what is it you're trying to sort out?"

"You know, I'm not sure. I mean, we finally found out the real story behind the stage brick falling, but we're left with a whole new set of problems."

"Problems?"

"I keep getting this nebulous feeling that there's a plot afoot. I couldn't exactly tell you what the plot may be, but I can't shake the feeling that the governor's life may be in danger."

Cameron spun his chair around to the computer table, put his plate down, and grabbed a nearby writing tablet. "Okay," he said, "It's see if we can sort this out." He started jotting down names.

"Okay, there's the auditorium staff: Mike the manager, George–or 'Trail Boss'–the technical director, Sheila the lighting director, Paul the stage manager, and Billy the stagehand. Oh yeah, and Jodie, the new box office manager.

"First Mike says he was in his office when the stage brick fell, then he fesses up and says no, he knocked it off, and then changes the story *again* and says his technical director did it."

Mary said, "Do you believe the final version of the story?"

"I'm not sure I would if it weren't for the bruise on George's shin. The coloration seems to indicate that it would have happened at about the time he says it did."

"So, are Mike and George part of your 'feeling' that Danford's in danger?"

Cameron pondered for a few seconds. "No. At least not directly. That whole 'tuba caper' is what got me into this, but I don't think that have any direct involvement in what's bothering me. Sheila's another story though. She's a real piece of work. Overblown sense of self-worth, thinks she has a good reason to hate Danford, and makes it obvious to everybody that she does hate him." He circled her name. "I'm going to keep her in the equation for now."

"I can understand that."

Cameron tapped his pencil where he had the next names written. "Billy and Paul. Neither one sets off any alarms. They've been good sources of information and that's about it. Now Jodie, I don't know if I should give her a red flag or not." He stopped short of telling her about Jodie and Mike's entanglement, but circled Jodie's name, saying, "She's not ringing any bells right now, but I'm not quite ready to strike her off the list."

"Okay, what about Mike?"

"Oddly enough, even though he's a haughty SOB, I trust him."

"Well, what about this nephew, Gus Danford?"

"I would have had Gus Danford on the list, for obvious reasons, but he's not a factor any mo–"

Mary said, "What?"

"Something just popped into my mind that I should make a note of. Hold on." At the bottom of his list of names, Cameron wrote, 'Who killed Gus?' He spun back toward Mary and said, "Okay, where were we? Oh yeah, the band members we've come across." He began writing again. "Lets see, I've got Phil the trumpeter, Jeff the drummer, Danford's niece Katrina and her friend Dolores on clarinet, and then Jerry Dale and Loretta Jackson on auxiliary percussion. Which reminds me, I'll be talking to Ms. Jackson in the morning."

"So we don't know yet if she'll be one of your red flags."

"Right. And then we've got Tuba John. I'm going to scratch him off the list of suspects because he got this whole thing going by being a near-victim. And I'll take Phil and Jeff off as well, because they've done nothing but help me and Ken. I'm not ready to take Katrina off the list quite yet, because all I know about her is that she's the Governor's niece. Right now, though, she and her friend Dolores don't stand out as potential problems. Out of all the band members, my most prominent red flag is Jerry Dale."

Mary said, "I still don't understand why Elliott doesn't want to pursue a search warrant on him."

"I don't know, maybe I misunderstood him about that. I'll try to get hold of him first thing tomorrow and see what's going on."

"I could tell that last call upset you, so that's probably a good idea."

Cameron shrugged. "Probably." He looked back at his list. "I'm not sure if I'm any further along than I was, but at least I've narrowed it down to some key suspects. Like I said, I'm not sure what I suspect them of, but at least I know where to direct my thoughts."

Mary got up and walked over to Cameron. "How about you rest your mind for a while and let's go to bed." She picked up his nearly untouched plate and added, "Do you want to have a bedtime snack first?"

Cameron grinned. "Nah. I'm good, thanks. Here, I'll take that to the dishwasher." He got it from her and went to the kitchen as she headed toward their bedroom. While scraping off his plate before putting it into the dishwasher, he wondered, *"Am I making a mountain out of a molehill? Have my 'adventures' gone to my head?"* He decided to follow Mary's advice and clear it all from his mind for the night.

Cameron stopped at the bathroom to brush his teeth, and when he came into the bedroom, Mary asked, "Why are you walking like that?"

"Like what?"

"Like you're favoring your left leg."

"Oh, that. Well, I had a little mishap at Jerry's place. Tripped over something in the dark and banged my shin a little."

"Let me see."

Cameron reluctantly took of his pants for her to see his leg. She fumed, "Banged it a little? Have you even seen your leg?"

Cameron looked down at the red, swollen protrusion on his leg and whistled. "No, I haven't. Guess I better put something on that, huh?"

"Get an ice-pack out of the freezer. And take a couple of aspirin. I swear, am I going to have chaperone you every time you go out?"

As he finished undressing, Cameron said, "No. I'll try to be more careful from now on." He went to the kitchen for the ice pack, got a couple of aspirin from the bathroom, and settled in to bed.

CHAPTER TWENTY

Cameron got to the office at eight-thirty on Wednesday morning so he could get himself settled before Loretta Jackson arrived. Right away, he texted Elliott and left a message for him to call, and then started perusing some pending files. At nine-forty, Loretta still had not arrived and he called the number he had for her. A message said that the number was no longer in service, so he gave up waiting and dove into his pending workload. When, at ten, Nedra buzzed to tell him that his nine o'clock appointed had arrived, he went to the lobby to greet her.

Loretta stood when Cameron arrived, and while she did not exactly tower over him, she was at least eye-to-eye with him. From a distance, she appeared to be in her early twenties, but when Cameron stood closer to shake hands, he could see that the face behind her ample makeup had the 'rode hard and put up wet' look often seen in addicts. He introduced himself and, as they walked back to his office, said, "You look familiar. Are you a Riverport native?"

She responded, "Been here all my life."

He said, "You're not any relation to Howard Jackson, are you?"

"As a matter of fact, he's my daddy."

"That's why you look so familiar. I know him from Rotary and I see him around town a lot, but I haven't seen since you were in middle school."

She sighed wistfully, "Those were good days."

As they walked to Cameron's office, a vague recollection sprang into his mind of Howard once lamenting over a daughter's troubles. Howard had not detailed the troubles, or named which of his three daughters had the problems, and Cameron now wondered if he had meant Loretta.

When they were seated, Cameron said, "Are you having any troubles? I tried to call you when you didn't get here at nine, and got a disconnect notice."

"Oh, yeah. Sorry about that. I, uh, just got a new phone, and it didn't dawn on me that you'd called my old number the other day. I completely forgot I was supposed to come see you today until about fifteen minutes ago, so I scrambled over here as fast as I could and didn't have time to call. Sorry."

"That's all right. I worried that something had happened to you. Well, let me give you some information about why I needed to see you. I understand that you and Jerry Dale play auxiliary percussion in the county concert band, is that right?"

"Yeah. I mean, we're not buddies or anything, but we both play in it. Why?"

"Apparently, somebody heard you and Jerry talking about a certain cymbal case that was found at the auditorium, and wondered if you remember that conversation."

"Umm, kinda. I mean, like, not word for word, but, you know, the gist of it. Am I supposed to be in some kind of legal trouble or something?"

"Not that I know of. I've been looking into what happened when that stage weight fell off the flyrail–"

"Oh man, that scared the crap out of me, it was so loud. You suing somebody over that?"

"No, somebody asked me to look into it is all. Anyway, some other safety concerns have come up because of the Governor's visit."

"Oh yeah, I heard about that. I think Katrina in woodwind's his niece or something."

"That's right. So, can you tell me what you can remember about your conversation with Jerry that night?"

"It wasn't much. We were settin' up and I saw this cymbal case that I didn't remember puttin' on the truck when I helped pack it the day before. I asked him if he knew anything about it and he got real funky–started asking me if I was accusing him of something. I told him to chill; all I wanted to know was if it was part of the stuff we're supposed to use, because I didn't recognize it. He right away said it wasn't ours and I asked should I look in it and see what it was, and he real quick said leave it alone, it might be a bomb or something."

"He talked about it being a bomb?"

"Yeah, but then he laughed real loud and said, 'JK' and I said that's not the kind of thing you kid about, and why would you even say something like that anyway, you know?"

"Let me ask you, did he ever look you in the eye during this conversation?"

"Now that I think about it, no. He looked all around the room and all, but didn't look right at me. But then again, He doesn't look at many people in the eye when he talks to them, if he even talks to anybody at all. Except Chip Eason."

"Chip Eason?" Cameron scribbled a note to check on Eason.

"Yeah, they're good buddies, and always making trouble. They're pretty immature, you know? Band director's always calling them out and keeps threatening to kick them both out, except everybody knows she won't because Chip's the best trumpet we got and if Jerry goes, Chip'll go."

"Did you ever do anything else about the cymbal case?"

"Nah. I had too much to do right then, and didn't even think about it until we got done rehearsin'. I guess somebody took it to the truck so they could load it with our other stuff. After the truck left, Jerry asked me where was the case, and he 'bout freaked out when I told him I guess it left with the truck."

"Did you ask him why it mattered to him so much?"

"I really didn't want to get into it with him, so I walked away."

"Did anything else about the cymbal case bother you, or catch your attention?"

Loretta hesitated. "L-Like what?"

"Like whatever drew your attention to it in the first place? Was it a different brand from other band cases, a different color or shape? Did it smell different?" Cameron stared intently at Loretta when he mentioned smell. He noticed a slight dilation in her pupils, but nothing determinative. Something else about her eyes seemed a little disturbing, or maybe challenging, though he could not quite decipher it.

Loretta said, "Um, yeah. All the equipment cases that belong to the band are stamped with the band's name, and this one didn't have anything on it."

"You didn't notice anything else peculiar?"

Again, Loretta's pupils dilated somewhat as she answered, "No, except it didn't have the band name stamped on it."

"Okay, have you noticed Jerry doing anything that seemed unusual to you?"

"I mean, he's always weird, so I guess everything he does is unusual, but I know what you mean. Probably the thing about the cymbal case is all I can think of."

"He hasn't said anything derogatory about the Governor?"

"Oh, well he's always bitchin' about politics and the way they're runnin' the state and all."

"Okay, let me ask you one more thing. Did you suggest to Katrina Knowles that she should invite the Governor to the concert?"

Loretta rared back in shock. "Me? Good heavens no. I hardly know her and I know less about Danford, so why in the hell would I do that?"

"I wouldn't know. Just following up on things I hear. Well, thank you, Ms. Jackson." Cameron handed her his business card. "If anything else comes to mind, please give me a call."

"Do you think Jerry might be planning to do something...I don't know...dangerous?"

"Can't say. We're looking into anything that might pose a threat, so don't read too much into it." Cameron stood to see her out. "Thank you very much for talking with me, and the best to you on the concert."

As Cameron saw her out his office door, she turned to him and said, "Oh, yeah, I do remember one thing. I overheard Jerry bragging to Chip one time about being related to Senator what's-his-name–the guy that's running for governor–for what that's worth."

"Buck Randall is the candidate's name. That is worth knowing, thank you."

Cameron followed Loretta to the front lobby, and when she left, he told Nedra, "When Ken comes back in, tell him I need to talk with him, please," and went back to his office to work.

After about an hour, Ken tapped on Cameron's door and peeked inside. "Nedra said you wanted to see me?"

Cameron set his paperwork aside and said, "Come on in. I talked with Loretta Jackson this morning, and she gave me some vital information."

Ken took a seat and said, "Great. What did she tell you?"

"First, she'd confronted Jerry Dale about the stray cymbal case in the auditorium and he acted pretty funny about it. But more importantly, she's heard that Dale may be related to Buck Randall, the senator who's running against Governor Danford this year."

"Whoa. That puts another slant on things, doesn't it?"

"It does in my mind. Mighty funny to have the governor's nephew doing funky things, and then winding up dead on one hand, and then a relative of Danford's opposition doing funky things on the other hand."

"Do you think Elliott knows that about Dale?"

Cameron punched his speed-dial. "One way to find out. I'll put you on speaker. I guess we're assuming that Elliott's still speaking to us."

After a few rings, Elliott answered. "If you're calling about Jerry Dale, we've already got him under arrest for the murder of Gus Danford."

Cameron said, "Still amazed at your mind-reading abilities. That's what we're calling about. And the fact that we think Dale could have it out for Governor Danford. I might have some evidence for you on the murder charge, by the way."

"How 'bout texting me with that info. But he won't be out on bail any time soon, so no threat to the Governor from him. We'll still keep a sharp eye out, but I think our main threats have been eliminated. Sorry about cutting you short the other day, but we were in the middle of the arrest. Listen, I appreciate everything you and Ken have done to help us out, but I don't think we'll need you on the security team any more. We'll still have the sniffer dog there and all, but I don't see so much of a threat now."

Cameron could think of nothing else to say, so he thanked Elliott and said good-bye. When he hung up, he said to Ken, "What do you think?"

Ken said, "You must be wearing off on me, because I've got a hunch it's not really over."

Cameron laughed. "Uh-oh. Guess I <u>am</u> wearing off on you. What facts give you that hunch?"

"I dunno. Too many loose ends, I guess. For one thing, we never figured out who left the message for you to back off. Everything points to Jerry, but when we went to see him, he didn't seem to have a clue about why we were there."

"Yeah, I caught that too. But <u>somebody</u> at the practice that night, had to have left the message, and it had to be somebody with access to my private land line. So, who would it be?"

"The voice kind of sounded male, but some women, especially the ones with with froggy-sounding voices, can sound male."

Cameron raised an index finger. "Wait a minute. What's that you said? Froggy-sounding voices? What does that mean?"

"I, uh, I mean, to me, it's women with a deeper, raspy kind of voice. You know the way heavy smokers sometimes sound?"

Cameron slapped the desk-top. "That's it! That's what's been rattling around in the back of my mind about that call. The voice didn't sound quite male, didn't sound quite female, but your 'froggy-sounding' female voice hits it on the head. And I think there's somebody we need to talk to asap."

"Who?"

Cameron picked up his desk phone and buzzed Nedra. "Ken and I are driving out to the auditorium. Not sure when we'll be back." He then said to Ken, "There's only one female we've talked to with that kind of voice. Well, I say we talked to her, but it was only me. I'm hoping she'll be at work today, since they'll be getting ready for the big concert tomorrow."

As they drove to the auditorium, Cameron told Ken about his interview with Jodie Miller, the box office manager. "She's got exactly the kind of raspy voice you're talking about, but I never made a connection until you brought up how somebody with that kind of voice can lower it a little more and sound like a male. Up to this point, I didn't think we needed to worry about her; just somebody screwing the boss and worried about getting in trouble. Now, it looks like she's played a good game of throwing suspicion off herself."

Cameron took out his phone and made a call. "Mike? Cameron Scott. Listen, is Jodie at work by any chance? She is? Good. I'm on my way out to see her. Yeah, I'll let you know after I talk to her. Make sure she's out in the lobby, but don't tell her I'm coming to see her, okay? Thanks, see you in a bit."

Ken said, "I take it she's working."

"She is. Oddly enough, Mike said she wasn't scheduled to come until tomorrow morning."

"Really? Think she's excited about Danford's visit?"

"Excited might not be quite the word for it, but yeah, I'd say her extra work hours have something to do with it."

At the auditorium, Cameron traveled up the circular drive in front of the building and parked. He and Ken hopped out and climbed up the short set of stairs to the front entrance, where Mike opened the door for them. Jodie stood behind the ticket counter on one side of the lobby, and when she saw Cameron, her faced paled. She immediately said to Mike, "Oh, I just remembered, I need to work on that batch of VIP tickets for the gala next month."

Mike said, "There'll be time for that. Right now, Mr. Scott and Mr. Benton want to chat with you."

Resignedly, Jodie stood in place while Cameron asked Mike, "Is there a place nearby where we talk with her privately?"

Mike pointed up the stairs that rose behind the ticket counter and said, "You can use her office up there. She'll show you the way."

Jodie hesitated, shifting back and forth as if she wanted to bolt, but finally came out from behind the counter and led Cameron and Ken up the stairs. Inside her office, she pointed out two chairs for them, and stood by her desk chair. She said, "What can I do for you gentlemen?" in a voice that was more or less calm, but a little shaky. Cameron could detect panic rising in her face.

Cameron said, "You remember our little talk the other day, at my office?"

"Y–yes. Did you have some more advice about that?"

Jodie looked back and forth between Cameron and Ken. Cameron assured her, "Yes, Mr. Benton and I had some discussion about our talk, and he agreed with my advice to you. He is under the same constraints about confidentiality as I am, so don't worry about that. But I have a little something different I want to go over with you."

"Not about me and Mr. Stevens?"

"No. About this." Cameron pulled out his phone and punched some buttons, and a voice came through the speaker, "Back off."

Immediately, Jodie's knees buckled and she flopped down into her chair, her face whiter than when they had entered the building.

Cameron said, "Ken and I have no doubt about this being your voice. What I want to know is, why?"

A few tears welled up into Jodie's eyes. She still looked like she wanted to run, but composed herself and said, "Oh, um, that. Jerry Dale put me up to that. He never would tell me why he wanted me to make the call, or even who he was calling. He, uh,...he said it was a prank on a buddy of his. I didn't think much of it at the time, but I can certainly see how it would seem suspicious, um, in light of all the goings-on the last few days."

"Did he say how he got my home phone number?"

"No, he...he didn't really say. He told me a number to dial and I dialed it."

While Cameron and Jodie spoke with each other, Ken busied himself looking at the pile of papers on her desk. One, in particular, caught his eye.

Cameron said to Jodie. "The call came from a phone with a 513 area code. Would you know anything about that?"

"It was Jerry's phone, but I didn't see the number."

Cameron punched a few more buttons on his phone. Within a few seconds, a muffled buzz sounded from somewhere within Jodie's desk. Here eyes shifted quickly between the desk and Cameron. He said, "Might as well answer it; it's going to keep ringing."

Jodie's hands shook as she pulled open a desk drawer, withdrew a flip phone, and punched a button on it. She immediately closed the phone and slammed it on the desk. "Damn, I can't believe he put that thing in here. I don't lock my office door very often, so Jerry must have snuck in here when I was someplace else."

Cameron gazed steadily at her and said, "Of course, that must be it. All right then, I guess that answers all of our questions. Thanks, and sorry to bother you."

"Oh, that's okay. I understand your concern. Glad I could help straighten it out for you."

Cameron and Ken walked out of Jodie's office and closed the door behind them. Cameron turned to see what her next move would be, but closed Venetian blinds covered the office door and window. They didn't filter out sounds though, and he thought he heard her talking on a phone in hushed tones.

They found Stevens in his office and Cameron told him, "I wanted to ask Jodie about a strange phone call I got a little while ago, and she had an answer. Didn't you tell me once that she came from out of state?"

"I don't think you and I ever talked about her, but she did move here a few years ago from Ohio, why?"

"I have a funny hobby of trying to pinpoint accents. Looks like I got pretty close on hers. Appreciate you having her available. How're things going in preparation for the big concert?"

Stevens rubbed the back of his neck and said, "Nothing much. Everything we do is being questioned and cross-checked by deputies and troopers who probably never set foot in a theater before. That's about it."

Cameron chuckled. "Ken and I might come to see the concert, if there's room in the audience."

"The band usually brings enough audience to fill about three-quarters of the seating. Even with the Governor here, I don't expect to be SRO, so come on over and bring a guest if you want."

"Thanks, I think we will. See you tomorrow."

They left the building, and as soon as they got into Cameron's truck, Cameron pulled out his phone and worked with it for a few moments. Finally, he said, "Thought so."

Ken said, "Thought what?"

Cameron turned the phone screen toward Ken and said, "I did a reverse lookup, and, sure enough, that phone with the 513 area code is registered to a Jodie Meuller, with an Ohio address. Looks like, for some reason, she anglicized her name to Miller before moving here.

I'm guessing that either she's unaware of how to do a reverse lookup, or didn't think that someone else would do it."

Ken said, "Good job. I think I found an answer to another question you had."

"What question did I have?"

"How somebody came up with your home number. Let me ask you, have you and Mary ever ordered tickets from this auditorium?"

"You know, as a matter of fact, we did see a good cover band here a couple of years ago, why?"

"I noticed that Jodie had a spreadsheet printout on her desk that showed patron information, including addresses and phone numbers. Think you might have used that home number when you ordered your tickets?"

"Holy crap. Great detective work, Inspector Benton. She got our home number from box office records. I'd say she's definitely the source of the threatening call. Next questions: "Why would she make the call in the first place, and is she actually a threat to Danford, or is there something else going on here?"

"And where do we start looking for those answers?"

"Let's do this. We'll go back to the office. You start checking social media under both her last names; I'll follow up with some of the contacts we've made so far. Who knows, she might be up to something that's got nothing to do with Danford's visit; something Elliott might be interested in but not our business. Maybe"

"You don't sound too convinced of that."

"Nope."

As soon as they got back to the office, Ken went back to his computer, and Cameron got on the phone. He first called Mike Stevens. "Mike, Cameron here. I said I'd catch you up on why we came in today, so here it is. I received a threatening phone call recently, and we've traced it back to Jodie."

"What!? Can't be."

"I'm afraid it can be. The call came into my land line at home, a number that very few people have. But she has access to your ticket-sale records, and Mary and I got tickets at Graves a few years ago, so she could easily find that number. In her office, I dialed the number that called with the threat, and lo and behold, a phone in her desk drawer started buzzing. Remember me saying I thought she came from out of state?"

"Yeah, and I said Ohio."

"That phone was registered to her when she lived in Ohio. And the voice on the call is nearly identical to hers. She tried to blame it all on a band member, but Ken and I know better."

"Well, damn. I don't get it. Why would she even do such a thing?"

"That's what we're trying to find out. Can you think of any reason she would have any connection with a percussionist named Jerry Dale?"

"The name doesn't sound familiar."

Cameron realized that word of Dale's arrest had not been released yet. "Well, I think he's connected to the suspicious cymbal case that got left on stage."

"The one with explosives residue?"

"That one. Looks like he's the one that brought it in. Try to think hard about whether she may have any connection."

Silence ensued for several moments, then, "There might...there might be something, but it's not much."

"Anything, at this point, could be much."

"If I tell you something, it stays confidential, right?"

"I can't promise the confidentiality a client would have, but I can promise that it would stay between us."

"I don't think anybody else knows about it, but Jodie and I have been having a, uh, a little fling for a little while. I mean, no big deal, and nobody here knows about it, but she came onto me pretty strong and I..."

Cameron thought, *"You just think nobody knows about it,"* but said, "Go on."

"Well, one time when we were...together...she admitted to me that some 'drummer' with the band, as she put it, had been pestering her to go out ever since they started rehearsing here. She said she didn't want me to be mad in case I heard about it."

"What did you tell her?"

"To be honest, I told her I didn't give a rat's ass. Like I said, we didn't have a real relationship, just some casual sex, you know what I mean?"

"So, you don't think she and this drummer are related to each other or something?"

"I doubt it. I mean, them being related would make him putting the make on her pretty awkward, wouldn't it?"

"True, but not unheard of. No other indication that they'd talked with each other much or socialized?"

"Not that I'm aware of. Do you think the two of them are planning something together? In relation to the Governor's visit, I mean."

"That's what I'm trying to figure out. Listen, do me a favor and don't mention our conversation to her, okay? I'd rather not get her guard up at this point."

"All right. I'll keep it to myself."

"Thanks. Talk to you later."

Cameron ended the call. He next called Sheila Rivenbark. When she answered, breathlessly, Cameron said, "Is this a bad time?"

"It's fine, but I can't take long. I've been on the lift trying to get the stage lights set. What's up?"

"I thought Trail Boss did all the lift work."

"I might have exaggerated a little about that. But anyway, what do you need?"

"I don't know if you would have even had a chance to observe what I'm going to ask, but have you noticed your box office manager talking a lot with one of the concert band members since their rehearsals started?"

"Jodie? You mean other than her usual flirting? Actually, her and Mike have been joined at the hip so much lately, I don't think she's had time to talk to anybody else. Then again, I'm not here full time, so who knows. No, wait, I did overhear her and one of the drummers talking one night."

"Talking about what?"

"I was in the shop looking for something, but kinda hidden behind some equipment, so they didn't know I was there. I heard him say something like, 'Everything's all set,' and she said, 'What do you need from me?' and he said 'Put it in the right place,' but then somebody else came in and they quit talking." Sheila snorted out a laugh, "I thought they were talking about doin' the dirty, you know, so I didn't think more about it."

Cameron laughed lightly and said, "I can understand that. And that's the only time you've heard the two of them talking?"

"That's it. I'm usually at the light board, in the seating section, so I don't normally hear what goes on backstage."

"All right, thank you very much."

"So, what's all this about?"

Cameron lied, "Still trying to make sure there's no more hidden dangers from falling objects is all. Bye."

Cameron ended the call and jotted a note about the Jodie/Jerry conversation. He started to dial his next call when Nedra buzzed him, saying, "Got somebody on the line for you. Wanna take it?"

"Do you know who it is?"

"No. They spoke almost in a whisper and asked for you."

"I'll take it."

Cameron hit the button for the caller and said, "Cameron Scott, how may I help you?"

A barely audible voice answered, "Mr. Scott, I need to see you."

"Who is this?"

"Meet me at 130 Crandall Road tonight at 7:30. By yourself.

Goodbye."

A click, and the call ended. Cameron buzzed Nedra. "Did you get a caller ID on that last call?"

"No, I'm sorry. Nothing showed."

"Okay, thanks."

As soon as Cameron hung up his call to Nedra, he heard a tap at his door. He said, "Come on in," and Ken entered, carrying some notes.

Cameron said, "Tell me what you found out, and I'll tell you about the call I just got, and then we're going for a ride."

Ken said, "Whoa, must have been some call. Anyway, here's the scoop on Jodie." He perused his notes. "Most of her posts are mundane, but she's gotten a lot of direct messages from one person with the screen-name 'Siss Boom' and another one 'L Boom'. There's also a few other noteworthy posts that either she's left or that somebody else put on her timeline. I couldn't open the DMs, so I don't have any idea whether they're anything for us to worry about."

"Siss Boom sounds like noises from cymbals and drums to me, but I don't want to read too much into that yet. What stood out in the posts that were visible to you?"

"Actually, most of them were reposts, all of them in support of Senator Randall, some against Governor Danford, and a lot of them pretty nasty. Here's screenprints of a lot of them." Ken handed Cameron a sheaf of printouts.

Cameron flipped through the printouts, and then said, "Wow, nasty is right. You know what? I think we need to get hold of Paula Fulton and see if she can dig into those DMs."

Paula Fulton, a private investigator who had recently helped Cameron and Ken crack a human trafficking case, answered Cameron's call on the second ring. "Hello counselor. You must have a serious problem. What can I do for you?"

"Hey, Paula. Serious is right. As usual, I've got lots of leads on something that might fizzle into nothing, or at least nothing I can take to law enforcement. But it might mean that somebody's trying to assassinate our governor."

"Whoa, sounds like your kind of case. Can't say I'm overly fond of Danford, but I despise Randall. He's dangerous. So, how can I help?"

"Fairly simple this time, but I need it in a hurry. If bad stuff's going to happen, I think it'll happen tomorrow. You up for it?"

"Buddy, you're lucky. Right now, everybody seems to be behaving, so I've got plenty of time on my hands. Give me the details."

Cameron said, "I'm going to put you on speaker phone. Ken's here with me and–"

"Hey, Ken."

Ken answered, "Hey, Paula."

Cameron continued. "I'm going to email you copies of some screen shots, along with somebody's email addresses, and the screen-name of two people who've been sending direct messages to her. I need to find out what's in those DMs. At this point, all I've got is a hunch. It's a pretty strong one, but for some strange reason, law enforcement still can't get warrants based on hunches."

"Not even your legendary hunches? Go figure. All right, send me what you've got and I'll get right on it. I can't guarantee an answer before this evening. Will that be okay?"

"The sooner the better, but that's fine. Text me as soon as you find out something, and email me your results as well. Hold on and let me see if Ken has anything to add." Cameron looked at Ken, who shook his head. "All right, he's good. Talk to you later."

When Cameron ended the call, Ken said, "Okay, now tell me about the call you just got."

"Ah, yes. I couldn't identify the caller because they whispered. I couldn't even tell their gender. Whoever it is, they want me to meet with them at 130 Crandall Road tonight, at 7:30. I figured we could ride out and see what's there while it's still daylight, if you're not too tied up."

"I'm good. Wanna pull the address up on gps before we go?"

"Good idea. At least we'll know the neighborhood." Cameron turned to his computer and typed the address into his gps app. When the map appeared, he zeroed in on 130 Crandall Road and went to street view. He and Ken both looked at each other in confusion. "Unless something's been built there recently, it's an empty lot"

Ken said, "Looks like mostly farm land around it. Sure you got the address right?"

"Positive. That's the one thing I could hear clearly. Well, let's go out and see what it looks like."

Cameron left word at the front desk that he and Ken would be gone for a short while, and they took Cameron's truck to the address. To their surprise, construction of a convenience store was well under way on the site. Ken said, "The photos on the app must have been taken several months ago. Looks like this store's been under construction for a while." A couple of brick-masons working on the store's front stared at Cameron's truck as it slowly drove past.

"Why does it not surprise me to see one coming in here," said Cameron. There seems to be one on almost every other road in the county."

Ken laughed. "Do you want to get out and look around?"

"Nah, there's not much to see. I do want to travel on this road some more though." Cameron drove forward.

"Looking for anything in particular?"

"A hiding place for a car. Your car, to be exact."

"I, uh..."

"I know I'm supposed to show up alone, but I'd rather have some backup, if you're game."

"As in hide my car down the road and sneak back here? Anything special I'm supposed to watch for?"

"I really have no idea. All I know is that if it's a setup, I want somebody around to call the law."

After they had ridden about a mile, Cameron did a 'K' turn and said, "Nothing but fields down this way, and nothing grown high enough to hide a car. Let's turn around and backtrack."

They passed the construction site again, and in less than half a mile, Cameron slowed and said, "That abandoned gas station looks like a good place. What do you think?"

"Drive around to the back and let's scope it out."

Cameron eased into the cracked and rutted concrete entry drive, and made his way to the back of the building. Ken said, "Head over there, to that old metal shed," pointing to a rusted, open-ended metal carport with solid sides. "Looks big enough to fit my car, but let's see what's inside."

When they got to the carport, Ken stepped out and took a better look inside the carport. He came back to the truck and told Cameron, "Perfect. There's some junk at the back end, but that's all. I'll have to allow time to park here and walk the distance to the construction site, so I guess that'd be about fifteen minutes or so longer than it'll take you to get to the meet site. Do you want to meet at the office before we come out?"

"Yeah, that's a good idea. I'll meet you there at 6:30. Meantime, we've still got a little time to do office work and then eat."

On the drive back to the office, Ken asked, "Any ideas on who your mysterious caller might be?"

"A few, but nothing to say for sure that's who it is. I guess the most obvious choice would be our friend Jerry Dale. Then there's our most recent person of interest, Jodie Miller."

"She's certainly a piece of work. Why do you suppose she came to see you? Do you think she really wanted advice about her affair with Mike Stevens?"

"Not really. I especially doubt it now. I get the feeling she tried to steer me toward suspecting him, but I don't know."

"I still have my doubts about Sheila Rivenbark. She seems awful shifty to me."

"That she does. Of course, it could be somebody altogether different about something unrelated to what we've been working on. We've been concentrating so much on what's going on at the auditorium that it seems like everything must have a connection."

Ken laughed. "That's true. Might be somebody calling about zoning problems with that store under construction, for all we know."

Cameron nodded, with a laugh. "Could well be. But I think we both know that somebody speaking in barely a whisper who wants to meet in a remote location at nightfall isn't calling about business problems. I guess we'll have to wait and see."

At the office, Ken and Cameron each tended to client business until closing time, and each went home for supper.

CHAPTER TWENTY-ONE

Over supper, Cameron told Mary about the mysterious call and that he would be meeting with Ken at the office at 6:30. Mary said, "A night-time meeting with who knows who in the middle of nowhere? Have you lost your mind?"

"Ken's going to be nearby to back me up and–"

"Why the hell don't you call Elliott to back you up? You know his deputies would be better equipped. Better yet, get Elliott to go."

"One: Elliott's got enough on his hands right now. Two: I don't want the possibility of patrolling deputies spooking off whoever I'm supposed to meet. And three: I'll be carrying."

"Oh great, Cowboy Cameron might get into a shootout, and widow Mary will have to pick up the pieces."

Mary's words sent a chill down Cameron's spine. He said, "I hadn't quite looked at it that way, but I understand your worries. Look, if I didn't have an overwhelming feeling that something catastrophic is going to happen tomorrow, I'd drop the whole thing, but I'm in one of those quandaries I've been in before. I don't have enough solid evidence to convince law enforcement to take action, but I've got so many warning bells jangling in my head that I can't ignore them."

Mary sighed heavily. "I know you enough to be sure that if I tried to tell you not to go, you'd take that as a challenge. All I'm going to say is, you better be careful, 'cause if you make if back, I might kill you for going in the first place."

Cameron reached out to hug Mary, saying, "I promise, I'll be super careful," but she pulled away.

Mary said, "I'm serious. I don't like this one bit."

Cameron wavered for a moment, torn between a duty to prevent inevitable harm to the governor and a duty to prevent inevitable harm to his marriage.

Finally, Mary reached out and took Cameron's hand. "Look, I knew when we married that you could be a pig-headed fool at times, and I also knew by then that your sense of justice could override your...sense. I want you to make me a promise."

"That being?"

"I want you to promise–cross your heart promise–that from now on you'll think these things through <u>before</u> they grow into such a big mess that you can't get out of them. You're not getting any younger, Cameron, and you can't keep running around playing superhero."

Her last words cut to the quick, but Cameron knew them to be true, recalling the difficulty he'd had climbing the auditorium stairs. He gazed deeply into her eyes. "Cross-my-heart promise. Sometimes I get so locked in to in a problem that I forget the world around me, and you're right, I've got to think before I swim, so to speak."

"All right. Go on, but please don't take any unnecessary chances, and call me when you're on your way home."

"I'll call, I promise."

Mary pulled him close for a hug. "You can be a pain in the ass sometimes, but usually, you're okay to be around, you know?"

Cameron laughed and leaned in for a kiss. Mary had her eyes closed, but he saw the beginnings of tear drops under her lashes. She hugged him tightly enough to nearly knock the breath out of him. In a few moments, she pulled back and said, "You need to go if you're going to get there in time. You've even got me curious about what's going on now, you big idiot."

Cameron ran a hand through her curly auburn hair and smiled. "I'll see you in a little while and give you all the juicy details. Love you."

"I love you too. Now go."

Cameron went to his home office safe and extracted two pistols, retrieved concealable holsters from a nearby drawer, and left. Ken was at the office when he got there, and he told him about the conversation with Mary, adding, "I've always known deep inside that my exploits have bothered her, but it's never struck home the way it did this evening."

Ken said, "Not too late to call this whole thing off, you know. I haven't had a chance to keep Mia abreast of all our comings and goings, but I get the feeling she wouldn't approve of this meeting either."

"No, it's...it's all right. I think we need to do everything we can to head off a disaster. But Mary's right; I can't keep this up. And it isn't fair to drag you into this, either. But here we are, and we may as well get it done. I brought this for you." Cameron reached into his glove compartment and took out the second holstered pistol. Ken said, "Seriously, dude? You think it's going to get that hairy?"

"Who knows? If my gut feelings are right, something big and dangerous is getting ready to happen, and there are dangerous people involved. So, yeah, it might get that hairy. It's got a full clip. Do you know how to operate one of these things?"

Ken laughed. "Our encounter with that Zero Tolerance group taught me that I needed some training, so yeah." He checked the safety before slipping the holster into his pocket. "And, by the way, you haven't 'dragged' me into anything. I'm a willing participant."

Cameron smiled and checked his watch. "All right. Time to go. I guess we need some kind of signal system so I know you're nearby. Cameron pondered for a moment. Let's see. Have you ever heard a whippoorwill at night?"

"Not that I know of. What do they sound like?"

"Kind of like their name. They aren't that common in these parts, especially this time of year, but here's the sound." Cameron whistled the 'whip-poor-will' sound and said, "Try it."

Ken tried the whistle and Cameron said, "Good ear. I think that's close enough. We'll hope whoever I'm going to see isn't an outdoorsy type. I saw a small grove of trees about a hundred feet from the construction site. After you get parked, walk to it and hide there. When you see me get out of my truck, do the whippoorwill whistle a few times so I know you're there. In the still of the night, it'll carry pretty well."

Ken practiced a few more times, and said, "Okay, got it."

"You won't have many places to go for cover when you're walking, so if any cars come by, try to act normal and keep going. If they slow down a lot, go back to your car. It's time for you to go now, so git."

Ken went to his car and left. About fifteen minutes later, Cameron took off toward Crandall Road.

A little before 7:30, Cameron pulled into the as-yet unpaved parking area of the construction site, turned off his headlights to let his eyes adjust to the darkness, and stepped out to look around. The masons had not quite finished the store's front, and pallets of bricks stood on the ground nearby. The remaining steel framework and sheet-metal exterior, along with the roof were done, but no windows, doors, or interior work had been installed. Various piles of construction materials adorned the lot.

The cool nighttime air made Cameron glad that he had worn a jacket. He zipped it partway and stood still, listening. He knew, from his early work as a state park ranger, that the term 'still of the night' was a misnomer; southern nights presented a loud chorus of assorted wildlife sounds. At the moment, he only needed to hear one soloist break through the chorus, and a plaintive whistle met his hopes. He smiled, his nerves settled somewhat by the knowledge that he had backup nearby, and he waved in the general direction of the nearby woods.

Cameron judged that the most probable place to encounter his caller would be behind the building, concealed from the view of passing cars. His way there was lit by a three-quarter moon, but he stepped gingerly; the recollection of his recent run-in with a tricycle fresh in his mind.

Behind the building, in an area shaded from moonlight by the building's shadow, he came to two side-by-side stacks of lumber and stopped. A distinctly unnatural click sounded somewhere nearby. Instinctively, he reached for his pistol, but a voiced hissed out, "Put your hands up. If I was going to do you harm, you'd be dead by now."

Cameron did as told. He was having a hard time pinpointing the talker's location and cautiously perused his surroundings. A barely audible scrape drew his attention to the right, where a door frame opened into the shadows inside the building. A figure emerged from the shadows with a hand outstretched. Although the moonlight was too dim for him to make out whether the hand held anything, he judged that the 'click' he had heard gave a good clue.

The figure came close enough for him to see that there was, indeed, a gun in the hand, a shaky hand, and as the figure drew close enough for him to see more details, he said, "I'm guessing you're Ms. Taylor. I'm Cameron Scott."

"Dolores, yes." She lowered the gun and continued, in a quavering voice, "I had to be sure nobody else could hear what I have to say. It could cost me my life."

Cameron said, "With no idea what I'd encounter, I brought a friend–"

Dolores quickly raised her hand again. "You were supposed to come alone, damn it."

"Whoa, whoa. It's all right. It's my law partner, Ken Benton. He knows about your call, and he's helping me."

Dolores looked like she might run any second, and Cameron added, "Whatever you have to say will be held in the strictest confidence by both of us. I think we're all working toward the same end, so please stay and let us talk with you."

Dolores's hand trembled while she tried to make up her mind, but she finally said, "All right, call him over." She brandished the pistol, adding, "but I'm not putting this away yet."

"Fair enough." Cameron called out, "Ken, come on to the back of the building."

Within a minute, Cameron heard Ken running toward them. When he got close, he slowed to a fast walk and then appeared in the moonlight, gun drawn. Cameron said, "Put it away. It's fine."

Ken reholstered the pistol and approached warily, saying, "I hope you're right. Who's this?"

"This is Dolores Taylor, Katrina's friend."

"Ah, of course. We talked on the phone. But why are we meeting here, like this?"

Cameron said, "Evidently, somebody's got her very frightened. I told her that we'd hold anything she'd like to share with us in confidence."

Ken said, "Absolutely."

From his vantage point, Cameron could see some of the roadway in front of the building. A car slowed down a bit as it went past the site, and then resumed speed as it traveled on. He thought, *Most likely wondering what my truck's doing out here at night.*" To Dolores, he said, "Please, talk to us."

Dolores looked back and forth between Cameron and Ken for a few moments before resolutely shoving her pistol into her coat pocket. "Okay, here it is. I get the feeling you've already been lookin' into Jerry Dale, right?"

"We've had him on our radar, yes."

"Good, 'cause you should. There's some other stuff you need to know, but I can't go to the cops with it or I'll be dead. Remember I told you on the phone that my mom's a county commissioner, right?"

"I remember."

"You gotta keep her outa this too, 'cause she ain't done nothin' wrong, okay?"

"All right. Go ahead.

Dolores drew a deep breath, held it for a few seconds, and then whooshed it out. Finally, she said, "Okay. Mom's got a special cell phone she uses for county stuff. Sometimes, if it rings or buzzes when she's not around, I look to see who it is, and if they leave a text, I read it. I know I'm not s'posed to, but I do anyway. So, I was at her house the other night, and her phone dinged, like it does when a text comes in. She was out for a while, so I took a look at the text, and it gave me a chill."

"What did it say?"

"It said 'Stay away from concert Thurs.' You know, like, Thursday. Then there was the letter 'L' after it."

"Had she planned to go to the concert?"

"I think about every politician in the county's planning to go, 'cept Randall's biggest supporters."

"Does that mean she is or isn't planning to go?"

"She can't stand Randall or anything he wants to do, so yes, she wanted to go and hobnob with the governor. But now she's afraid to."

"Do you have any idea who 'L' might be?"

"Not really. I mean, there's a Louise on the board, but it could be anybody."

"Do you know Louise's last name?"

"No. I only hear mom talk about her once in a while, and it's not usually nice."

Ken said, "Do you think Louise wanted to keep her from hobnobbing?"

Dolores said, "I hadn't looked at that way. I seemed like a warning to me."

Cameron said, "So it could be political infighting, or it could be a serious threat."

Dolores said, "There is another thing."

"Okay, shoot."

Never in a million years would Cameron have guessed that those words would have been taken literally by anyone. Before Dolores could answer, two loud cracks pierced the night, nature's chorus ceased, and Dolores dropped to the ground. Cameron and Ken ducked behind the lumber pile, drawing their pistols on their way down. They both turned to the direction of the report and cautiously peeked over the woodpile.

Hearing rapidly retreating footsteps, Cameron told Ken, "See if you can catch up. Don't put yourself in danger, but find out where they went. I'll call 911." He speed-dialed as he spoke, and let the dispatch center know his location and what had happened. As he talked, he checked on Dolores's condition. He saw a crimson circle widening under her left side, but he could not tell the exact location of her wound and did not want to move her before EMTs arrived. Already, he could hear the distant warble of sirens.

While they waited, Dolores haltingly said, "More to tell you...in case I...,

Cameron said, "Ssh. Try to stay calm. Help's on the way.

"No, I need to tell you. A second text came." She paused to take a labored breath.

Cameron took off his jacket and placed it under her head, saying, "Take it easy, they'll be here soon."

Dolores persisted, her voice growing weaker, "The other text... from Randall's office! That was...number on phone." She gasped several times.

Cameron said, "Please, don't try to say anything else. The ambulance is almost here." He did not have to say more. She closed her eyes and went limp, her chest rising and falling, but barely.

The rescue vehicle pulled in behind Cameron's truck, and he yelled "Over here." He heard people scramble toward him and yelled "here" once more. When they got to him, he said, "Careful, there's a pistol in her coat pocket. Her name's Dolores Taylor. She should have some kind of ID on her. "

A breathless Ken showed up behind the EMTs. Cameron got out of the way of rescue personnel and pulled him to the side. "Any luck?"

Ken took a few moments to get his breathing under control and said, "He, or she, got a good head start, so I didn't get a good view. But I got to see the license plate on the car they got into, parked about a half mile down the road."

"Damn, I saw a car slow down as it passed here. That was probably it," said Cameron.

Ken continued, "The good news is, I got a shot of the license plate." He took out his cell phone and pulled up the photo.

"Oh wow, I can't believe it's readable. Good work." said Cameron.

By this time, the EMTs had stabilized Dolores enough to load her into the rescue rig. One nodded his head toward the sound of an approaching siren and said, "You can tell <u>them</u> the details."

Cameron said, "Think she'll be okay?"

The other EMT said, "Too soon to tell. Gotta go." She jumped into the driver's seat and the rig sped away.

Cameron told Ken, "I guess we don't look too dangerous. She didn't even wait around to see if the law was going to run us in."

Ken said, "I don't think they had time to waste. Meantime, here <u>is</u> the law."

A vehicle, siren still blaring, skidded into the gravel parking lot and stopped in front of Cameron's truck. He and Ken both raised their hands and walked toward the cruiser. Two deputies jumped out and one barked out, "Is one of you Cameron Scott?"

Cameron gave a quick, surprised look toward Ken and responded, "That's me. How did you know that?"

"Sheriff told me to ask. Said it sounded like something you'd be in the middle of."

The deputies could not see Cameron's stomach shake as he

engaged in a silent laugh but he said, "Okay if we put our hands down?"

The other deputy had run a quick check of the building and its perimeter and returned to the first one's side. The tag on the first one's jacket said, 'Priggemeier' and the other's said, 'Bevan'. Bevan said to his partner, "All clear. Any statement?"

Priggemeier said, "We haven't got to that yet." He directed a question to Cameron, "Give me a quick rundown. Who shot the vic and why are you two here?"

Cameron said, "First, we've got some information you might want to follow up on asap. Ken, give them that plate number."

Ken took his phone and showed them the picture of the license plate, saying, "This might help answer your first question. This is the shooter's tag number. They might still be on the road."

Bevan wrote down the tag number and immediately hit a button on his collar mike, calling for an immediate 'BOLO' and urging "Caution, the occupant or occupants may be armed and dangerous." As soon as he finished, another vehicle eased into the lot, its siren silent but blue lights flashing.

Elliott Grainger stepped out of the car, head shaking. "I knew it."

Cameron tried to effect his most innocent look, leaving Elliott unimpressed. Elliott asked Priggemeier, "Got a statement yet?"

"No sir, they gave us a tag number, and were sending a BOLO out when you got here."

Elliott said to Cameron, "This better be good."

Cameron said, "I got a call to meet somebody here at 7:30. You've all but told me to get out of this case, and at the time, and I couldn't see any reason to bring you in on it, so I agreed to come out here."

"Who were you supposed to meet?"

"Turned out to be Dolores Taylor, a clarinetist in the concert band. She said she had some important information for me." Bevan went straight to the cruiser and started typing on a laptop inside.

"Okay, so you got here about 7:30, right?"

"Right."

"Both of you?" Elliott pointed to Ken.

"I let Ken off down the road, and he walked over to that grove. She said for me to meet her alone, but I wanted backup."

Elliott patted Cameron's waist and pointed toward the pistol hidden there. "In addition to that backup?"

"Uh, yeah." Cameron quickly added, "I've got a permit to carry. Anyway, like I said, I didn't know what I'd be coming up against. In fact, Ms. Taylor surprised me with a drawn weapon. Once I assured her she was safe–"

"With you two, that's a matter of conjecture, but go ahead."

"Well, anyway, Ken joined me and she started to tell me about some information she had."

"What information?"

Cameron looked at Ken. "We both promised that we wouldn't draw her 'informant' into this, but I don't see a way around it, under the circumstances. In fact, I suspect EMS has already contacted the person in question, so I'll tell you that Dolores is Commissioner Taylor's daughter, and Commissioner Taylor is her unwitting informant."

Elliott put his hand to his face. "Sharon Taylor, one of my best supporters on the County Commission, and you two let her daughter get shot? Great."

"Wait a minute. She's the one who called this meeting, not me."

"All right, what happened next."

"She told me that her mother's commissioner phone dinged when her mother was out, so she checked to see who left a message. The text said, "Don't go to the concert," with an 'L' for a signature and nothing else."

"Is that it?"

"She started to tell me something else when she got shot."

Priggemeier's two-way squawked and he answered it, "Go

ahead." A voice said that the car with a license number matching the one Ken had given them had been stopped in Riverport, and the officer was holding the driver for questioning." Priggemeier looked at Elliott, who said, "Ask the officer to hold 'em 'till we can get there." Priggemeier relayed the message.

Elliott said, "So, did she get a chance to say anything else?"

"Only that the phoned dinged again, and showed that the message came from 'Randall's office'." Then she passed out. Only Randall I could think of right off is the Lieutenant Governor."

Elliott told Cameron and Ken, "All right, we're going to take it from here. I'll keep you posted on anything we find out." He poked each one on the chest and added, "And you're both back on security. I might be crazy for doing it, and I'll probably catch hell from some quarters, but I might as well keep you two where I can keep an eye on you. Be at the auditorium at ten tomorrow morning."

Cameron and Ken both nodded, dumfounded. Priggemeier and Bevan both looked at each other quizzically, but said nothing. Elliott told the deputies, "Follow me," as he climbed into his car, and then they all left.

Cameron said to Ken, "What just happened?"

Ken said, "Damned if I know."

Cameron said, "I guess I'd better report back to the boss before word of this shooting gets out. Wanna come to my house for a late snack and skull session?"

"Sure."

Cameron took Ken to his car, and they drove back to Riverport. On the way, Cameron called Mary and told her, "Ken and I are fine, but the contact who wanted to meet with me isn't in such good shape."

"Oh my gosh, Cameron, what the hell happened? Are you sure you're okay?"

"I'll give you the details when I get home. Ken's coming to the house, too. Do we have any beer in the refrigerator?"

"Since when did you start drinking beer?"

"I haven't; it's for Ken."

"I think I've got most of a six-pack left."

"That'll be good. And I've got some Canadian left; do we have any ginger ale?"

"About half a bottle, in the refrigerator."

"Okay, see you in a little bit. Love you."

"Love you too. I think. I'll let you know for sure after I hear the details."

Cameron laughed, uneasily, and ended the call.

At the house, Cameron took Ken straight to the home office and Mary came in with the six pack and bottles of Canadian and ginger ale. She already had glasses set out. She stopped in the middle of putting the beer down and said, "Holy crap, Cameron, is that blood on your sleeve?"

Cameron looked down at his sleeve and said rather absently, "Well damn, it is." He added quickly, "It's not mine."

"Don't tell me it's—"

"It is. Let's settle in and I'll tell you the whole story."

Mary grabbed a beer for herself and gave one to Ken. Cameron poured himself a Canadian and ginger ale, and they sat facing each other.

Mary opened with, "I know I saw you leave here with a jacket on. Where is it?"

Remembering that he had propped Dolores's head up with his jacket, Cameron said, "It's at our meeting site. Let me tell you what happened and you'll understand why." He then told her about Dolores and the as-yet unknown shooters, and his jacket becoming a 'pillow'.

Mary asked, "Is she still alive?"

Cameron said, "Don't know yet. I imagine Elliott will let us know soon." His phone buzzed and he said, "Maybe that's him now." He looked at the screen, saying, "Nope, it's Paula." He answered it with, "Hold on and I'll put you on speakerphone. Mary and Ken are

-154-

here with me." He got the phone set up, he put it on the coffee table in front of him and said, "Okay, go ahead."

Paula said, "It took me a while, but I got most of what you needed."

Cameron said, "Great. Could you get an ID on Jodie's mysterious correspondents, 'Siss Boom' and 'L Boom'?"

"I got 'Siss Boom' and still working on the other. Does the name Oren Danford ring a bell?" Paula's question elicited stunned silence. She said, "Hello? Are you still there?"

Cameron said, "That's the governor's brother. His son, Gus, died here a couple of days ago under suspicious circumstances."

Paula said, "Oh yeah, the Governor's nephew. Wasn't there something in the news about him committing suicide?"

"Turns out it was a murder."

"Oh. Sorry to hear that."

"Us too. Did you get a chance to dig into those DMs?"

"That I did. I think you're going to want to see those, so I'm texting the results straight to you. You should be getting them any second."

On cue, Cameron's cell phone buzzed, but he went straight to his desktop computer to pull up the texts. He read what she had sent, with Ken reading over his shoulder. "Whew, that's some scary stuff. Thanks, Paula."

"No problem. Let me know if there's anything else you need."

"Will do. Bye."

Cameron ended the call and said to Mary, "Let me sum up what Jodie's been getting from Oren Danford. Essentially, Oren's been plotting to kill his brother, or rather, to have him killed." He dialed Elliott's number while he spoke. When Elliott answered, he said, "I'm with Ken and Mary and I've got you on speakerphone. I'm forwarding some information we've uncovered that I'm sure you'll want to act on right away." He sent the messages Paula had found as he continued, "Any word on Dolores Taylor?"

Elliott said, "She's out of surgery and in ICU. There's been some damage to her innards, but nothing that couldn't be fixed. She lost a lot of blood, so it'll take her a while to recuperate."

"I take it she hasn't been able to talk yet."

"Not yet. The hospital knows we need to speak to her, but they want to be sure her vitals are stable first."

"I understand."

Elliott fell silent for a moment, but then said, "Holy crap, Cameron. I don't want to know how you got this information, but I'm getting on it right now. Thanks."

"Glad to help. Keep me posted, okay?"

"Will do, as soon as I can. Bye."

Cameron hung up and said, "I think we got his attention."

Mary said, "Sounds like it."

"I guess we've done what we can do for now. Maybe Danford will finally figure out it's not safe to come here."

Ken said, "Or maybe the concert can be postponed again, at least long enough for this threat to be taken care of."

Mary said, "I like that idea. Take away the reason for the threat to be carried out."

"Seems like that would be the sanest solution," said Cameron. "But 'sane' and 'politics' seldom seem to meld, so I don't see it happening. I guess we can contact Mike and see if postponement's a possibility. And we can suggest it strongly to Elliott so he can pass the word. Tell you what: Ken, how about you text Mike and I'll text Elliott with the idea and we'll see where it leads."

Mary said, "It's getting late. How about we get that done and get some rest?"

Cameron said, "I get the hint. Ken, see you in the morning. I get the feeling that tomorrow's going to be a grueling day."

After Ken left, Mary told Cameron, "I know you; you're going to run this through your mind over and over. I'm going to bed, but please don't stay up late, okay?"

"You do know me. I wish there weren't so many unanswered questions, but maybe if I hash it out long enough, I can come up with some solutions. Meanwhile, I promise I won't be too late."

Mary went to bed, and Cameron made himself comfortable on his office chair, in front of his computer, trying to fit the pieces of the puzzle together.

CHAPTER TWENTY-TWO

At two in the morning, Mary woke Cameron, still in his desk chair, head back, mouth open. She said, "Your snoring woke me all the way back in the bedroom. Come on to bed."

Cameron first responded with a dazed, "Huh?" His mind then cleared enough for her words to sink in, and he got up and dutifully followed her back to their bedroom, mumbling something about a repetitive dream he'd been having.

"I kept trying to pick my way through a giant maze, with obstacles at every turn. Dolores Taylor kept popping up, but always at a distance, trying to point the way out. Every time I'd catch up to her, she'd zoom away and point a different direction. I finally caught up to her, and she was about to tell me something, but her eyes were glazed and her mouth kept moving up and down with no words coming out. Then you woke me up."

"I'm not surprised, as much as you've been obsessed with this mess. You need to get a good night's rest and clear your mind."

"You're right, but whatever's going to happen will happen tomorrow, and that doesn't give us much time to sort it all out."

"Fine. If you want to go back and work on it, go ahead. But lay on the couch or something so you don't start snoring again. You're lucky I'm off tomorrow, or I'd really lay into you about snoring me awake."

Cameron could tell by her tone that Mary was not joking. He thought it best not to aggravate her mood any more that night and settled into the bed with her. It did not take long for him to drift back to sleep.

Five hours later, Mary shook Cameron awake again. He said, "Huh? Wha–?" and stared at her through bleary eyes.

"Damn it. Now you better be 'specially glad I'm off today. I stayed awake half the night thinking about what's been happening, and your dream, and I don't know what else. And, I think I've got some of the pieces put together."

Now fully awake, Cameron pulled himself up, resting his back against the headboard. "I'm listening."

"Let me get some coffee first. Don't go away." Mary flung the covers back and disappeared through the doorway.

Cameron decided to make use of the time until she got back, and went to the bathroom. As he got back into the bed, she reappeared, two coffee cups in hand. She put one on his night-stand and circled round the to recline on her side of the bed. She said, "Okay, here's what I've pieced together. We've learned that the governor's own brother wants to do him harm, right?"

"According to his own brother's emails, that's a given."

"And we know that Oren's been working with Jodie Miller to put that plan into effect."

"Jodie's one we know about. And I presume that Elliot's got her in custody by now. Who knows who else is in on it."

"Jerry Dale, for sure. And he's also in custody."

"I've been thinking about that. We know that the lighting director, Sheila whats-her-name–"

"Rivenbark."

"Rivenbark, yeah. She's been pretty vociferous about hating the governor, right?"

"Right."

"So, that gives us one more suspect."

"Us?" Cameron laughed.

Mary smacked Cameron's arm and said, "You've drawn me into yet another one of your messes, so it's definitely 'us'. There's nothing much against Sheila to justify an arrest, but she looks like a prime suspect to me."

"True. In fact, I need to call Mike Stevens first thing to see if he had a relationship with Sheila."

"You don't think he'd lie?"

Cameron thought about it for a moment. "You know, he's pretty conceited, but I think he's basically honest, so no. He might be reluctant to tell me, but I'll remind him that it's vital to the security of his facility."

"His facility being what comes before all?"

"Exactly. His 'baby'. Any other thoughts?"

"Didn't you tell me that the technical director's out on parole?"

"George Hall? Yeah, but I haven't seen him as a likely suspect. Why would you?"

"Think about it. He's the one who would know that building inside and out, and would know how to conduct a 'surprise attack'."

Cameron took a sip of his coffee while he thought about Mary's words. "That's good point, but that would also make Mike a suspect, wouldn't it?"

"Yes, but Mike's not on parole. Do we even know what George went to jail for?"

"Assault, as far as I know. Keep in mind that he and Mike both have been looking for suspects."

"Or at least that's what they said. George could have volunteered to do that to throw suspicion off of himself."

Cameron took another long sip. "Okay, let's suppose George is our man. What would be his motive? I mean, we know that Jodie is in league with Oren Danford and Jerry Dale's been arrested for killing the Governor's nephew. But what interest does George have?"

"I did a little research while you slept–and I couldn't–and found a few things about George Hall. It turns out he's related to Senator Randall."

Cameron almost dropped his coffee cup. "How in the world did you find that out?"

Mary took a turn at coffee-sipping and then said, "Remember you told me that George's assault conviction took place in Rowan County?"

"That' right. I forgot about that."

"I started looking through Rowan online records, and came across a newspaper report about his initial arrest. Since Rowan is Randall's home county, I guess the reporter thought the story'd get more attention if he mentioned his relation to Hall."

"Randall didn't post bail or provide him with a lawyer or anything?"

"There wasn't any mention of it."

"It must have been a pretty serious assault if he had to serve jail time plus go on parole."

"That they did mention. Evidently, he got in a bar fight and broke some guy's jaw. They also mentioned that he'd had previous scrapes with the law."

"Hmm. Good digging. That does put a different perspective on it. I can't remember if I've told you or not, but apparently Jerry Dale is also related to Randall in some way. Sounds like we have a whole Randall mafia right here in River City."

Cameron's phone buzzed. He picked it up off the nightstand and unplugged the charger before answering. "Good morning, Elliott. What's the news? Mind if I put you on speakerphone? I want Mary to hear. Okay, hold on." Cameron switched to speaker and put the phone on the bed between Mary and him. "Okay, go ahead."

Elliott first said, "Hey Mary," and she told him hello. He then continued, "I'm afraid our young lady is still in ICU and unable to talk yet. I'm already at the auditorium getting my deputies organized, and we ran a preliminary sweep of the building. Mike Stevens has been very helpful in showing us places we didn't even know existed. Lucky's gone through and sniffed everything, and didn't hit on anything. We'll make another sweep after the band gets here. Anything new from your end?"

"As a matter of fact, we do have some news. I'll let Mary tell you what she found out." Cameron gave Mary a nudge.

Mary said, "It might not amount to much, but I did some digging and found out that George, the technical director, is somehow related to Senator Randall."

"Whoa. We didn't even have him on our radar."

Cameron said, "Might not amount to much, but it's somebody else to keep an eye on. Add Jerry Dale to the list of Randall clan members we've got, and it sounds like we could have a serious plot going here."

"You bet."

"Oh, and I think Jodie, the box office manager's deep into it, too. She's been having some serious online conversations and direct messaging with Danford's brother, Oren.

"Listen, when do you think you and Ken can get here earlier than ten?"

Cameron looked at the clock on his phone and did a mental calculation. "I'd say about nine or so. Is that all right?"

"That's great. See you here. I'll tell the crew to look out for you."

"Okay, later."

Cameron ended the call and told Mary, "Looks like I better get up and at 'em." He swung himself out of the bed, shower bound, and called Ken to let him know when Elliott expected them.

After Cameron grabbed a quick breakfast, he scooted over to Mary's side of the bed to give her a hug, saying, "I appreciate your investigative help. Are you coming to the concert tonight? Might be a chance to meet Governor Danford."

"I'll come to hear the band. I want to see how they do with 'The Old North State'. What time do they start?"

"Doors open at seven and they play at seven-thirty. Mike's already supposed to have seats saved for you and Mia. That's assuming the whole thing doesn't get cancelled, which I hope it does."

"Okay, let me know. I'd love to see Mia again."

"Okay. Love you. Bye."

CHAPTER TWENTY-THREE

A state trooper stopped Cameron at the drive leading into the auditorium loading dock and said, "Could I see your ID please?"

Cameron pulled out his driver's license. The officer looked at it, consulted a list on a clipboard in his hand, and said, "I'm sorry, this area is restricted to auditorium employees and security personnel."

"I'm supposed to be cleared by Sheriff Grainger, along with my law partner, Kenneth Benton."

The trooper looked at a clipboard again and shook his head. "I don't have you or Mr. Benton on my list, and my orders come from my sergeant, not the sher–" The trooper put a finger to his ear and cocked his head, listening to something. He then pushed a button on a mic clipped to his shirt and said, "Ten four." He said to Cameron, "Somehow my sergeant knows you're here, and he says you and Mr. Benton are cleared, so..." The trooper stood back and waved Cameron through.

Cameron's view of the loading dock ahead showed why the trooper's sergeant knew he was there. Another trooper stood on the dock beside Elliott; both them looking toward him. He pulled into one of the few spaces not filled by law enforcement vehicles and a telecommunications trailer and walked over to the dock, saying, "Good morning, gentlemen," as he climbed the stairs.

Elliott said, "Good morning counselor." He nodded toward the trooper standing beside him and added, "This is Sergeant Dennis Crowley. He's in charge of safety for the Governor's visit today. I've told him about how you and Ken have been helping me."

Crowley extended a hand to Cameron, saying, "Appreciate the input. Sheriff Grainger tells me that you've helped him round up some potential perps, and that helps make our job a lot easier. We're keeping an eye on the technical director, but he's not otherwise on our radar. So, it looks like we're at normal threat level today."

Elliott added, "We've made a full sweep of the premises, including the sniffer dogs, and nothing caught our attention."

Ken bounded up the steps to the dock and joined the others. Cameron said, "Looks like we've made ourselves superfluous. Sergeant Crowley here, and Sheriff Grainger, tell me that there's not much threat to the governor."

Elliott said, "You're welcome to run your own sweep, if you'd like. I know you two have your own funny way of looking at things, so it wouldn't hurt. We got ID tags for you." He handed each of them an official identification tag hanging from a neck-lanyard.

Cameron said, "We'll talk about that, but first, do you have any idea where Mike Stevens is at the moment?"

Elliott said, "No, but I can find out real fast." He pressed a button on the mike attached to his shirt and said, "I need a twenty on the auditorium manager." Within a few seconds, someone answered, "He's in is office right now," and Elliott responded, "Good, thanks."

Cameron thanked Elliott and he and Ken made their way to Mike's office.

On seeing Ken and Cameron enter, Stevens stood and held out his hand to greet them. "To what do I owe this honor, gentlemen?"

Cameron said, "I've got a question that might embarrass you, but I need to find out whether to worry about one of your staff members."

Stevens cocked an eyebrow. "Um, okay. Which staff member."

"Sheila Rivenbark. Might you have had a little... 'fling' with her at some time?"

Stevens' face reddened. "I'm not sure why it's anybody's business, but she did come on to me pretty strong a few months ago and I might have given in to her charms. Do you think there's any connection to what's been happening?"

"Maybe. I know you're familiar with her hatred toward the governor, so it's possible she could pose a threat to him during today's visit."

"Believe it or not, I have given that a thought, and that's why I'm going to be at the sound board today, instead of Trail Boss, to keep an eye on her."

"What does Trail Boss think about that?"

"It doesn't matter what he thinks. That's how it's going to be done."

"And what will he be doing?"

"He'll be stage managing, at stage left by the curtain pull."

"Does he do that often?"

"No. He's usually at the sound board."

"I take it he's pissed. How much will the curtain get used?"

"None. But he'll get over it."

"Did you know that he's related to Senator Randall?"

Stevens blanched and looked unsteady for a second, but regained his composure and said, "I did not know that. Do you feel like he poses any kind of threat?"

"We don't know at this point, but at least one of us will be keeping an eye on him during the concert. Is he here now?"

"He came in at eight, with the rest of the crew. Do you want to talk to him?"

"No. In fact, do me a favor and don't let him know we've been talking about him. Meanwhile, Ken and I are going to check things out, at the invitation of the sheriff. Do we need you to unlock anything??

"I've already unlocked every door we have, for the sheriff and troopers to conduct their sweep. Most of them will be relocked before the band gets here."

"Okay. Thanks. One more thing."

"What's that"

"Did you remember to hold a seat for my wife, and…" Cameron looked toward Ken, who nodded, "…and Ken's lady friend Mia for tonight? They'll be happy anywhere."

"I did. Tell them to give the ushers their names when they get here. Anything else?"

"No, that's all, thanks. See you in a bit."

When they left Stevens' office, Ken said, "I think he found it a bit presumptuous that you'd remind him about your reserved seating after giving him the third degree."

Cameron laughed. "If he wasn't such a pompous ass, I wouldn't have done it that way. Now, let's get back to Elliott." Back at the workshop, they found Elliott conferring with some of his deputies.

Cameron waited for Elliott to take a break and said, "Can we talk about the work you and your folks have done so far?"

Elliott said, "Sure, hold on." He gave some quick directions to his deputies and said, "Okay, let's go to the green room. Do we need Sergeant Crowley here?"

"Probably not. Let's get talking and we'll see."

"Okay."

In the green room, Cameron said, "There's no point in us being redundant as far as searching goes. You and the sarge have a whole lot more experience than we do in that respect. Why don't you give me a quick recap of where you've been, and Ken and I can take it from there."

Elliott said, "Appreciate the compliment. You wouldn't believe how many nooks and crannies there are in this place, upstairs, downstairs, under the stage, over the stage, and every place. Bohn and Lucky have been there all the way, and nobody found anything unusual. By the way, did you get what you needed from Stevens?"

"Made sure he'd reserved a couple of seats for Mary, and Ken's friend Mia. And found out he's been playing around with his lighting director."

"Really? How'd that come about?"

"I asked him. I heard some rumors that he'd been picking flowers in his own pastures, so to speak, and I wanted to see if the flowers included an avowed Danford hater." Cameron purposely left off mention of the affair between Jodie and Stevens, since that information had come to him confidentially. "And to top it off, he's going to run sound right beside her during the concert. He claims it's to keep an eye on what she's doing."

"Great, one more thing to worry about. I'll let Sergeant Crowley know that we'll probably need to station somebody at the tech table. Where to for you?"

"I dunno, Ken and I will have to talk about it. Cameron looked at his watch. "Guess we'd better get movin'."

Elliott got a call on his radio and said, "Gotta go. Let me know if you find anything."

Cameron said to Ken, "Need another break or are you good?"

Ken said, "I'm good. Where to next?"

Cameron said, "I was going to ask you that. You're the one who's familiar with theater layout. Can you think of anywhere that the law enforcement folks might have missed?"

"I'd like to look around the grid, if that's all right with you."

"Where's that?"

"You remember the mesh 'ceiling' above the flyrail, way up over the stage?"

"Oh, yeah, up in the nosebleed area. Lead the way."

They made their way to the flyrail staircase, Ken let Cameron lead the way up the stairs at his own pace, until they got to the top. From there, they walked over to the flyrail and circular staircase, and Cameron paused.

Ken said, "I'll go up on my own, if you're not comfortable."

Cameron looked up the staircase for a few moments and resolutely said, "I can do it. Let's go." He immediately wound his way up the stairs until he got to the top. Stepping off onto the grid itself gave him pause again. As Ken had said, he could see straight down forty feet to the stage floor. He raised his eyes and resolved to keep them raised while they finished exploring. He asked Ken, "Now what?"

Ken said, "I want to check out a few dark corners, including that entrance." He pointed to a dark rectangle on the far side and strode across to it. Cameron gingerly followed, still refusing to look down. The rectangle, an opening about five feet high and three feet wide, extended downward into blackness. Rungs attached to its right-hand wall led downward into the abys. The florescent brightness that had lit their way thus far did not find its way down there.

Grabbing a topmost rung and ducking into the opening, Ken said, "Do you have your pocket light?"

Cameron said, "Right here," as he fished in his pocket to find it. He handed it to Ken, who shined its beam downward. Cameron could then see that the 'abys' only extended around seven feet down to a floor, with a doorway to the left.

Ken said, "Be right back," while he climbed down the rungs to the floor and disappeared through the door. In a moment, Cameron heard him say, "Okay," from somewhere and then saw the flashlight beam shine through the doorway, followed by Ken, who climbed back up the rungs and squeezed his way back through the opening to the grid floor.

Ken said, "Nothing but mechanical rooms over there." He and Cameron checked a couple of dark corners before he pronounced, "Nothing up here. The only other place I can think of is the FOH rail next."

When they got back down to the flyrail, Cameron looked down at the stage once more, thinking, *"Doesn't seem quite so high, now."*

They walked back off the flyrail, across the concrete floor, and up to the platform and door for front-of-house lighting. Ken swung the door open, and flipped a light switch. The area had a tinge of bleach smell to it, and Cameron asked, "Does fresh laundry get stored up here for some reason?"

Ken answered, "Not to my knowledge. I mean, that's not a regular theater practice."

Cameron eyed the steel mesh walkway, similar to the flyrail, that stretched out in front of them for more than twenty feet. Unlike the one for the ropes, this one had a solid covering under it. To the right, a window-like opening, nearly as long as the rail itself, provided a view down toward the stage. Thick steel rails and poles lined the walkway on that side, with various lighting fixtures affixed to them, all angled down toward the stage to different degrees.

Cameron held tightly to a horizontal rail and leaned forward enough to look down. A flash of vertigo nearly sent him reeling when he realized that he stood suspended about forty feet above the first few rows of seating. He regained his equilibrium by focusing on Ken, a stationary object at his level. Next, he turned his attention leftward, toward a vast field of superstructure that raked upward into the darkness. He told Ken, "That space looks huge."

Ken said, "That's the gridwork and cables for the ceiling tiles. It's all suspended from the roof. You can walk out there, but only if you know exactly where to step and where not."

Cameron pointed to the walkway on which they stood, and said, "Uh...is this just suspended from the roof too?"

"Afraid so. But it would just about take an earthquake to make it fall."

"Still, I don't think I'll jump up and down on it." He looked back toward the superstructure. "What are those things sticking up that look like cans?"

"That's the recessed lighting over the audience. You can see some of the wiring cables snaking all over the place."

"You know what, it's giving me the willies knowing that we're just hanging here. Let's go back down."

They went back to stage level and found Elliott in the green room, with Crowley. Elliott asked, "Find anything new?"

Cameron answered, "We focused on the grid over the stage and the front-of-house rail, but we didn't see anything. Although, I thought I smelled bleach when we went to the FOH rail. Did you tell us that Deputy Bohn got up there with Lucky?"

"He did, but they didn't detect anything."

"Might have been my imagination. Anyway, we're done."

Crowley said, "We've got another round when the band and their equipment get here, and then again when the audience arrives. We'll scan them and make sure absolutely nobody brings in anything bigger than a small purse."

Elliott looked at his watch and said, "Speaking of band members, they should start getting here soon. All right, let's keep our eyes open and get on with our jobs." They walked out to the loading platform in time to see the band's box truck coming down the drive. Elliott called for deputies and Crowley stopped the truck. Before it could back into the dock, deputies checked under and around it, and inside the cab. At the dock, unloaded items got a preliminary inspection by a deputy, and a good sniffing by Lucky.

Security directed all arriving band members to a side entrance, where deputies searched them and told them to report to the stage with their instrument cases. Each case received a thorough inspection and a sniffing by Lucky. One band member murmured to another, "What–do they think we're a bunch of terrorists?"

During the unloading and search process, Cameron and Ken contented themselves with watching the various band members for any suspicious mannerisms or facial expressions.

At length, the band got the go-ahead to set up for rehearsal, and they busied themselves with arranging chairs, assembling instruments, and tuning.

During the rehearsal time, Elliott called Cameron and summoned him and Ken to the green room for a meeting with Sergeant Crowley. At the meeting, Elliott ran his hand through his hair. "Best we can tell, everything's safe and sound. But let's remember that we'll have some people here who've expressed their contempt for the governor, and two in custody who seem to have been genuinely plotting against him. And we still don't know who their cohorts are. The Governor's due in–" Elliott checked his watch "–two hours, and all we can do is hope nothing really bad pops up."

Pointing to Crowley, he continued, "Meanwhile, mine and Dennis's crews will need to check every audience member who comes in. Let's talk to Stevens about that." Elliott got on his radio and asked one of his deputies to hunt down Stevens and ask him to come to the green room. Within a few minutes, he arrived and Elliott said, "Have a seat. We need to talk about surveillance, and checking out incoming audience members. For one thing, how often is that side entrance with the vestibule used?"

Stevens said, "It depends. For ticketed performances, we keep it locked and our ushers check people in at the front doors."

Elliott said, "Oh crap, ushers. What time do they come in?"

"About an hour before show time."

"Do they come in through the front doors?"

"Normally, yes. We get them all together and give instructions."

"Good. We can get them all checked out as soon as they get here. Back to the side entrance. With the vestibule there, it'll be a good place for the Governor to come in." Elliott asked Stevens, "Can we lock those doors so nobody can get in, but people can get out?"

Stevens answered, "Fire codes require us to have that kind of lock, so yes."

"Good. We'll lock it and post a deputy there to watch it."

"All right, I'll notify the staff, if that's okay."

"That's fine. They need to know the protocol. Also, you'll need to keep a block of seats available for the Governor and his entourage. As far as I know, they'll want to sit at the front of the auditorium. I imagine Dennis will want a couple of his troopers in there too, is that right?"

Crowley answered, "Right. I'll let them know where to sit.

Elliott went over the rest of the instructions, then looked at Ken and Cameron. "Anything else?" Both of them shook their heads and he said, "Good, let's get back to work."

Elliott and Crowley left the room and Cameron said, "Well, okay then. Mike, you can get back to directing your staff, and we'll take a late lunch break. Sounds like the band's done rehearsing. Are they taking a meal break?"

"I don't think so. They're probably too nervous to want to eat. From what I understand, the cops are taking a meal break in the event center soon, so the band's supposed to hang out on stage or in the shop until they're done, then they can go sit in the event center."

"I'm sure you love having that crowd hanging around your shop."

"I already okayed it. We don't have much to do back there right now."

"Good. All right, we'll see you in a bit."

Stevens left, and Cameron said to Ken, "While 'the cops' eat, let's see where we can get some fast food's around here. They got up to leave, but Elliott poked his head in the door, saying, "Sorry, forgot to tell you. You're part of security, so you're invited to come eat with us in the event center."

Cameron said, "Thanks. We'll see you there." He turned to Ken and said, "That'll save us a trip. Please tell me that I'm not the only one who thinks this is all insane. Red flags are flapping themselves right in our faces, we have at least two people on staff here who have good motive to do harm to the governor and all we can do is watch them, and we have a Governor who's taking up the macho banner on the dare of a loony opposing candidate."

Ken said, "No argument from me."

"Unless Elliott has something else for us to do, you and I are going to keep a close eye on our two main suspects throughout the concert, okay?"

"I agree. Do you want Rivenbark or Hall?"

"Why don't you park yourself in the back of the seating area and watch Sheila, and I'll park myself in the wings and keep an eye on George. Damn! I 'bout forgot about Jodie. Wonder where she'll be." Cameron speed-dialed Stevens. "Mike? Do you know were Jodie's going to be during the concert?"

Stevens answered, "She said she wanted to go home once we got the audience in, and I told her that would be okay."

"Is that standard practice?"

"Not necessarily. But after hearing what you've said, I thought it best not to have her here anyway."

"Good thought. Okay, thanks."

Cameron ended the call and they made their way to the event center, finding a seat at one of the round tables that had been set up. Shortly, two delivery people from a nearby sub shop brought in boxes of subs, chips and cookies and set them on a long plastic table on one side of the room. A cooler with soft drinks sat at one end of the table. Not long after that, a wave of uniformed men and women streamed in and helped themselves. The auditorium staff joined them shortly after. Ken and Cameron made their way over to the table and picked from the ample remaining food.

While they ate, Ken and Cameron both texted their mates to let them know that everything was fine.

At about 5:30, Danford and his entourage showed up. Sergeant Crowley invited Danford to meet with some key safety personnel before being seated, and they all gathered in the event center. Crowley again emphasized to Danford the possible dangers present in the auditorium that day. Danford replied, "I understand completely, Sergeant, and once again, I have faith in your and Sheriff Grainger's abilities to secure this building. You understand, Sergeant, that anywhere that public officials go these days can be subject to some sort of attack. I can't let such threats paralyze my ability to make public appearances, especially in an election year."

Crowley said, "Yes, but–"

Danford said, "No buts, Sergeant Crowley. I'm confident that you are all doing a thorough job. Please show us where we'll be seated."

Crowley gave up arguing, and led Danford to the front-row seating area that had been marked off. Danford frowned, pointed to a section of seating almost directly in front of the sound and light boards and inquired of one of his aides, "I think the acoustics would be better back there, don't you?" The aide agreed.

Mike and Sheila had been sitting at the tech boards, fiddling with controls. Cameron could not quite interpret the looks on their faces. He figured that Mike didn't care for his apple cart being upset, but Sheila? Did he detect a hint of panic in her eyes. And did her eyes dart up to the front-of-house lighting area, or did he imagine that? He did recognize the hatred in her eyes when she looked toward the Governor.

Cameron also found it particularly odd that a familiar member of the band had wandered back onto the stage about the time the Governor came in. When Danford announced the change of seating, Cameron heard her say "Damn" to herself and spun his head to look. He caught her gazing at the front-of-house lighting, but when she saw Cameron looking at her, quickly turned her attention to something else.

Stevens turned to Rivenbark and said something that Cameron could not hear, and she started fumbling with the light board. Most of the lights in the seating area dimmed considerably, and then a bank of ceiling lights over the tech board and surrounding seats brightened, highlighting the new area that Danford had pointed out. Danford immediately looked toward the board, smiled, and gave a 'thumbs-up' signal. Stevens, in turn, smiled broadly. Cameron noticed that Rivenbark rolled her eyes.

The auditorium lighting came back full and Danford said, "I see the staff are on top of things. Let me go back and thank them." He asked Crowley, "Do you know their names?"

Crowley said, "Mike Stevens is the auditorium manager. He's handling sound tonight. And the young lady at the light board is Sheila Rivenbark." Danford tilted his head for a second, as if in recognition of her name, but then shook it and walked up the aisle and over to the table. When he got there, Sheila and Stevens stood and held out their hands, but Danford bypassed Sheila, held his hand out to Stevens, and said, "Nice to meet you, Mr Stevens, I appreciate the little touch you just added. I'm assuming that's for when I'm announced?"

Stevens said, "Absolutely, sir." He pointed to a microphone attached to the sound board, "I'll make the usual pre-show announcements from here, and I'll be sure to welcome you and your group."

Danford smiled broadly and said, "Very good," and shook Stevens' hand one more time. In passing, he nodded toward Sheila, tossing off a curt "Thank you," as he walked back down to the front of the auditorium. Cameron saw the look of contempt on her face, and pictured her head smoking like a steam engine.

When Danford rejoined the security team at the front of the auditorium, he said, "I believe we have enough time for me and my group to grab a quick bite to eat. Sergeant Crowley, any recommendations?"

Crowley said, "I'm afraid the pickings are slim around here, sir. The only thing very close is fast food, although I believe a locally owned luncheonette might still be open. Would you like me to call?"

"Yes, I'm for locally owned whenever possible."

Crowley found the number, and called, then said, "They're open until six-thirty, sir. I believe if we leave now, we should be in plenty of time. She said they're not that busy right now."

Danford told an aide, "How about seeing if my niece can break free to join us. She's probably backstage somewhere."

Ken told the aide, "I can take you back there if you'd like."

The aide said, "That would be good, thanks." Ken led him to the stage stairs and they disappeared behind the wing curtains.

Shortly, the aide reappeared, saying, "She appreciates it, but she's afraid she'd get back too late to be in position for the start of the concert. She said she'll see you after."

Danford, looking a bit perturbed, bustled toward the exit, saying, "Let's go." The rest of his group followed suit, with Crowley bringing up the rear.

Cameron said to Ken, "Let's catch a quick breather." They went to the green room to relax for a while, and Cameron took out his phone to check messages. Mary had sent a text asking how things were going. He texted an 'okay' back, and let her know to check with the ushers about seats for her and Mia. The next message came from Paula Fulton. It read, *"Still trying to dig up who 'L Boom' is. Almost there."*

Cameron showed Paula's text to Ken and said, "What do you think?"

Ken said, "How long ago did she send that?"

"About ten minutes ago. I'll let her know to keep digging. Although, something about the screen name is tickling part of my brain." Cameron texted back to thank Paula and to let him know if she found out more.

They had left the door to the green room open, and an attractive middle-aged woman in a black dress walked in and plopped down, wiping her brow. She looked at them and said, "Hi, Margaret Hoffman. Do you work here?"

Ken said, "No, we're sort of a part of the security detail for today." He held out his ID tag. "I'm Ken Benton and this is Cameron Scott. Are you with the band?"

"I supposed you could say that. I'm the conductor for this concert."

Cameron said, "Very nice. I guess you've been with them throughout rehearsals?"

"Throughout. It's been nice, except for the smartass trumpeter and drummer—my two troublemakers. If they aren't interrupting practice with idiot jokes, they're arguing with me."

"Would that be Chip Eason and Jerry Dale?"

Margaret's eyes widened. "Yes. Do you know them?"

"Only heard about them."

"Thankfully, Mr. Dale dropped out at the last minute. I worried that Chip would quit at the same time, since he's our best trumpeter, but he's still with us. He's calmed down quite a bit since Jerry Dale left."

Cameron thought, *"Elliott's doing a good job of keeping Dale's detention under wraps,"* and said to Margaret, "Is Mr. Eason here now? I need to talk with him."

"Oh dear. Is he in some sort of trouble? If so, please let him at least finish the concert."

Cameron laughed. "Oh no, we only like to ask him some questions. Shouldn't take but a minute. Do you know where he might be at the moment?"

"They let everybody go over to the event center, where they could sit down. He should be in there with everybody else. Do you know where that is?"

"We sure do. If you'll excuse us, we'd like to go talk to him now."

"Certainly. It's been nice talking with you."

"Same here."

They left for the event center and Cameron explained to Ken, "Loretta Jackson brought up Eason's name when I talked to her at the office. I never got a chance to follow up with him, so now's the perfect time."

At the event center doorway, they stopped to survey the crowd. Most of the musicians sat in small groups, animatedly talking among themselves. Cameron assumed that the musicians segregated themselves according to their instrument types, so he looked for the one trumpeter he knew, Phil Pritchard, who sat with a group on the far side of the room. He approached Phil and said, "Hey, good to see you again. Can you introduce me to Chip Eason?"

Immediately a young man seated nearby spun his head around to look at Cameron. Phil said, "Chip, come over here. Somebody wants to chat with you."

Eason stood up and warily approached. Cameron said, "Hey,

Cameron Scott, and this is Ken Benton. Can we talk for a minute?"

Eason said, "I guess. Will it take long? We're supposed to be on stage in about five minutes."

Coincidentally, George Hall showed up at the entryway, held up five fingers and announced "Five minutes." Before leaving, he slowly perused the room, his gaze fixing on the percussion section for a moment before he moved on.

Ken told Cameron, "That's part of his job as stage manager, to give warnings about show time at certain intervals."

Cameron said, "Ah, thanks." To Eason, he said, "This won't take long." Pointing toward a remote corner of the room he added, "Let's step over there, it looks quieter."

When they got to the corner, Cameron got right to the point. "I heard from Loretta Jackson that you and Jerry Dale are tight. Is that right?"

"Whaaat? Why would she say that? We both kid around a lot during rehearsals, but that's about it. I'm kind of a cynic, so I do, like, dry humor. Jerry says lots of sixth-grade type nasty stuff and pisses people off a lot. Other than that, I hardly know him. In fact, I'm glad he dropped out; I don't think anybody'll miss him."

"You don't hang out or talk with each other online or anything?"

"Hell no. I don't even know why he dropped out. I mean, I heard a rumor that he's in trouble with the law, which wouldn't surprise me, but that's all I know about it."

"All right, Mr. Eason, thank you very much. Have a good concert. I hear you're an excellent trumpeter."

Eason's eyes brightened for a moment. "Thank you. Can I go now?"

"Sure can."

Eason hightailed it back to the trumpet group in time for George Hall to appear in the doorway again, announcing, "Places."

The musicians streamed their way out of the room toward the stage, and Cameron and Ken took another exit toward the seating area.

On the way, Cameron said, "This is getting curiouser and curiouser. I wonder why Loretta described them as best buddies?"

Ken said, "Maybe Eason lied to keep himself out of trouble."

"That could be. In the meantime, let's get you to your corner."

In the hallway leading to the seating area, they passed a fire alarm, and Cameron said, "I think this is the closest alarm to where you'll be. Keep it in mind, I get a feeling we might need it."

"Seriously? You think somebody might set a fire?"

"Not necessarily that, but we might need to clear the building fast if any surprises pop up."

At the doorway to the seating area, Elliott met them and handed each a walkie-talkie with an earplug, saying, "The earplugs have never been used. Stick it in your ear and keep up with our traffic. You can position yourselves where you want and if you spot anything, let us know. Got it?"

Both of them said, "Got it," as they each took a walkie talkie from Elliott.

Stevens had blocked off the balcony, anticipating less-than-full attendance, which left the downstairs seating area close to capacity. From the doorway, Cameron could see the backs of Mary and Mia's heads a few rows back from stagefront. He nudged Ken and pointed to them.

The band was already on stage, some of them still shuffling to their seats. Cameron hurried down a side aisle to get backstage, and positioned himself in the stage-left wing, not far from George Hall, who stood beside the curtain pull with little to do but wait around. Cameron imagined how useless he must have felt.

Precisely at 7:30, the house lights dimmed and the audience hushed. Stevens' voice sounded on the speakers, welcoming the audience and giving some routine information about emergency exits, turning off cell phones, and the like. He briefly introduced the college president, who stood and waved, then a circle of light brightened near the middle of the seating. Stevens, in his best 'announcer' voice, said,

"Ladies and gentlemen, we'd like to welcome the Governor of North Carolina, the honorable Philip Danford."

The band played a short fanfare while Danford rose and turned in all directions, waving to the audience. Some audience members applauded loudly, some barely clapped, and some sat and watched. Cameron's eyes were on George Hall and on the band members. Out of all of them, one caught his attention. Loretta, at the timpani, darted her eyes back and forth from where the governor stood, to the front row of seats, and back. He could not decipher the look on her face. Was she was calculating something? At length, she shrugged and smiled, and looked back to her timpani.

The lights dimmed again, and Stevens announced, "and now, the conductor of Fullwood County Concert Band, Ms. Margaret Hoffman."

The entire audience applauded as an area of the stage lights brightened. Margaret entered, bowed, and took her place on a small platform in front of the band. Stevens then announced, "Please stand for our national anthem." The audience stood, Margaret conducted the band in the anthem, and the audience all sat and settled in.

A microphone and stand had been set up next to the platform, and Margaret leaned into it to announce the musical theme for the evening: 'Down Home in Carolina,' and the name of the first tune. For the next forty-five minutes the band played a mix of old and new folk tunes, each one introduced by Margaret with a bit of background about the song. Thunderous applause followed each selection.

While the band played, Ken kept careful watch on Stevens and Rivenbark, as they worked the boards. Low lighting kept him from seeing Sheila that well before Danford's introduction, but he thought her hand shook as she pulled the lights back down afterwards. He scanned the rest of the room and noted a deputy standing guard next to a set of doors on the left that lead to the vestibule, and another at the right front doors that led outside.

At the end of the set, Margaret let the audience know that there would be a fifteen minute intermission. She directed the band members to stand en-masse, and they all walked off the stage through the wings.

Sheila brought up the seating area lights and audience members stood to stretch their legs or get to the lobby area restrooms. When most of the audience had cleared, Governor Danford stood, along with his entourage. Cameron had come on stage enough to see Danford motion to one of the ushers, who came over to him. They conversed for a moment, and the usher led Danford to the left-side double door that led backstage. Two troopers and some of his entourage followed him.

CHAPTER TWENTY-FOUR

As soon as Danford disappeared through the backstage doorway, George Hall bolted upstage to the double door that led into the shop. Cameron slipped into the shop behind him, intent on seeing if Hall did anything unusual or suspicious, in light of 'The Old North State' being the first song to play after intermission. Hall wandered among the band members, saying a word or two to some, but mostly peering about as if looking for something, or someone.

Governor Danford and his entourage stood at the far end of the shop, with Katrina Knowles. An aide spoke to a nearby stagehand, who pointed them in the direction of the green room. Hall watched them leave, but did not follow.

As he carefully scanned the room, Cameron spotted Loretta Jackson near the back exit door, next to a young trooper stationed there. She held two fingers in a 'V' near her mouth and pointed to the door. The trooper hesitated for a moment, but relented and opened the door for her to go out to the dock.

Cameron looked for Hall, and saw him staring intently toward the same door. At that point, Cameron sidled over to the trooper, showed his ID, then asked, "Aren't you supposed to be keeping people from leaving?"

The trooper looked Cameron up and down and said, "Pretty much so, but if somebody's dying for a smoke, I'm not gonna stop 'em, know what I mean?" He winked and patted a shirt pocket, where Cameron could see the outline of a cigarette pack.

Cameron uttered an absent "Mm hmm" and walked away. He texted to Ken about his current location and Ken texted back, *"In lobby, keeping an eye on things."*

He texted back, *"Good. Checking backstage. Watching George Hall and Loretta Jackson. They may be up to something. Stay at back left, near alarm for 2d half, okay?"*

"Got it."

Before long, Hall called out, "Five minutes," and moved toward the green room. Cameron followed, adroitly threading his way through clusters of musicians. He got near the green room in time to see George duck his head in to call "Five minutes."

Cameron slipped behind a wing curtain, not wanting George to see him, and when George headed back to the shop, followed him there. Band members still congregated in the shop, waiting for a call back to the stage, but Cameron did not see Loretta among them; nor did he see the trooper. He edged over to the exit door and stepped outside, where he saw Loretta leaning against a guardrail, not smoking, and the trooper puffing away and talking, or rather flirting, with her. She fiddled with something attached to a coiled plastic bracelet on her wrist. Her fingers covered most of the object, but Cameron had some idea of what it was.

Cameron casually said, "Tech director gave a five-minute warning a little bit ago. Just thought you'd like to know."

Loretta responded, "That's okay; got no timpani in the first song. I'll slip in right after that. Thanks, though."

Cameron jokingly told the trooper, "Watch her," but, with his back to Loretta, narrowed his eyes, hoping the trooper would understand that he was serious. Unfortunately, the trooper gave no indication that he caught the hint. He said to Loretta, "Okay, well, see you when you get back in place."

Cameron stepped back inside the shop in time to see Hall pop his head through the stage door and holler, "Places,." after which the musicians hastened through the stage doors on both sides of the shop. Cameron felt torn between staying in the shop to watch for Loretta and going back to the stage to watch George. He finally chose to go back to the stage.

Soon, Margaret announced, "Ladies and gentlemen, we'll be adding some waltz numbers for the second half of the concert. I believe our special guest will especially enjoy our first selection, "The Old North State."

Cameron heard murmurs and applause from the audience, and when the sounds died down, the music started. Oddly enough, someone Cameron did not recognize stood behind the timpani.

About halfway through the song, the door from shop to stage flung open, and a breathless Loretta Jackson rushed into the wing, muttering, "What the hell?" She stood listening for a few more bars, then she whipped past Cameron to the doorway at the end of the ropes, mumbling, "No no no no,". George, from his position by the curtain, dashed out the doorway behind her. Cameron followed, texting to Ken, "*Alarm! Flyrail. Loretta.*" When he got to the hall, he looked left in time to see the back of George's right foot passing through the stairway door.

The piercing squeal of the auditorium alarms nearly drowned out Elliott's voice on the walkie-talkie as he shouted, "Who the hell pulled that alarm? Somebody find out NOW! Let's get these people out so they don't run over each other. Dennis, you got the governor covered?"

Cameron said to himself, "Oh Crap," and yanked the walkie-talkie from his belt. While rushing up the stairs, he rather breathlessly said, "That was us. I'll explain later." Whatever Elliott said in returned got lost amid the chatter, alarm shrieks, and other cacophony in the auditorium.

As Cameron got to the landing leading to the second flight of stairs, he heard footsteps behind him. He turned and saw Ken bounding up, skipping every other step, and moved aside for him to zoom past.

Ken reached the flyrail level first, where the FOH rail door stood open. George Hall stood in the doorway, his back to Ken. Fearing the worst, Ken jogged up the steps to intervene, not prepared for the sight that greeted him. The interior lights were off, but in the dimly lit area beyond George, Loretta Jackson frantically paced back and forth, peering into the darkness of the superstructure, screeching, "Three-quarter pulse, what the hell." Hall inched his way toward her, shouting, "What the hell are you doing?"

Loretta glared back at him, her wild eyes almost unearthly looking–scarier than anything Ken had ever seen–and she shrieked, "Don't touch me! It's not working, it's not working, where is it?" She ran at Hall and shoved him backwards, and then climbed up on a wooden plank that had been laid across two struts, and crouched there like a wild animal, peering hard into the dark void. She screeched, "Somebody moved it, Damn it. Where is it?" to no-one in particular.

Ken flipped the lights on as Hall lunged at Loretta and tried to wrestle her off the shelf. She kicked him away and started climbing her way into the superstructure, groping about. She still screeched, most of what she said now unintelligible. Hall gingerly stepped his way toward her. She reached a black bundle wedged into an angle of bracing and snatched it up, but her foot slipped and she teetered sideways. Hall grabbed at her shirt but she kept falling, grabbing his arm on her way.

Ken ran toward them, hoping to get hold of an arm, a leg, or anything to pull them to safety, without success. Light poured through a gaping hole in the ceiling tiles as Loretta and George both fell through. George groped for something to hold onto but only reached the electric cable for a ceiling light fixture. Ken watched it and the fixture disappear downward, the cable stretching taut. The cable held for a second, but with a loud snap and shower of sparks, it gave way.

Ken could only see what happened next in his mind's eye, as he heard a short duet of male and female screams, followed by a sickening thud and crunch. He pulled out his walkie-talkie and said, "Need bomb squad and EMS at front of seating area, stat."

Presuming that Cameron had already made his way to floor level, Ken rushed down the stairs and into the auditorium. He felt a brief wave of nausea at the gruesome sight in front of him. At front and center, George and Loretta lay, bent and tangled over a section of seats, surrounded by debris from the ceiling. Loretta had landed under George, her neck bent at an unnatural angle, her eyes still open but seeing nothing. George still grasped the cable, the light fixture dangling at the end of it. Loretta's lifeless right hand clung tightly around the black bundle. Part of its outer covering had rolled back and Ken's heart skipped a beat when he saw a red light blinking through the hole.

Emergency personnel ran down the aisle and Ken immediately told them, "I think that black bundle's a bomb. Let's wait for the bomb squad. And I don't think I'd use radios right now."

The few minutes it took for the bomb squad to arrive seemed agonizingly long. They ordered Ken and rescue personnel out of the building and worked on gently prying Loretta's fingers loose to remove the bundle. They placed it into a bomb-resistant container and raced out the side exit with it.

The EMTs rushed back inside to worked on the tangled bodies, and Ken followed. He heard an almost imperceptible moan and realized that, despite the severity of his injuries, George had survived the fall.

Ken stepped away from the conglomeration of emergency workers, having time at last to wonder where Cameron had gone. From the back of the auditorium, a shaky voice cried, "Cameron?" He looked back to see Mary and Mia running down the aisle, with Elliott in close pursuit. Mia rushed to Ken and nearly knocked the wind out of him with a tight hug. Mary grabbed his arm and said, "Where's Cameron?" Ken looked around him and said, "I..I don't know. I thought he came downstairs before I did."

At that point, the walkie-talkies crackled and a somewhat broken-up transmission came through, saying, "Need EMS upstairs." One of the EMTs looked to Ken, who had given the 'no radio' order. Ken said, It's okay, bomb's out of here. The EMT radioed, "Need another unit." Someone answered, "Where?" and the first one answered, "Not sure, but it's upstairs." The second one responded "10-4." The walkie-talkie at Ken's belt crackled again, this time the message coming through clear, "Tell EMS it's top floor on the side with ropes. One male, breathing, otherwise unresponsive."

While one of the EMS workers relayed the message, Mary shouted, "How do I get up there?"

Ken said, "I'm not sure if—"

"Damn it, I know who they're talking about. Show me where!"

Ken told Elliott, "Sounds like he's up by the fly rail. I'll go with her. Can you guide EMS when they get here?"

Elliott responded, "Can do. Go."

Ken told Mary, "Follow me." He took her to the bottom of the flyrail stairway and said, "You go first. It's two flights up." He followed her as she rushed up the stairs to flyrail level. In a dark corner, a state trooper knelt over a motionless form. Mary gasped, "Cameron!"

The trooper said, "He's the one I talked to on the loading dock. This is how I found him when I got up here."

Ken said, "This is Mary Scott, that man's wife. EMTs are on their way up."

Mary knelt down beside Cameron and cradled his head in her arms. Her voice shaking, she whispered, "Hang in there, Boo, help's on the way."

The trooper said, "I don't know if somebody hit him or what."

Two EMTs burst into the room and Ken gently touched Mary on the shoulder, saying, "We need to give them room. She reluctantly stood and moved across the room with Ken and the trooper. The EMS personnel worked on Cameron, and at length, one of them turned to the trooper and said, "We've got him stabilized, but we'll need help getting him down the stairs."

Mary said, "Can you tell what happened?"

"No evident signs of trauma. Can't say 'til a doctor checks him out, but it looks like maybe a heart attack."

Mary gasped and muttered, "I tried to tell him..."

The EMTs strapped Cameron onto a stretcher, and Ken and the trooper both moved in to help carry him down the steep stairs. Mary followed close behind. When they got him to the seating area, another EMT waited with a gurney, and they gently laid Cameron on it before rolling outside to a waiting ambulance. Mary, Ken and Elliott followed behind them, but they sped away so fast, Mary did not have a chance to get into the ambulance. She started to panic, and Elliott said, "Come with me. He took her to a nearby patrol car, put her in the front seat with the surprised deputy, and said, "Follow the EMS rig." The car took off, blue lights flashing and siren blaring.

CHAPTER TWENTY-FIVE

A week after the concert, Elliott, Ken and Mia huddled with Mary in the Scott living room. Mary lamented, "I tried to tell him that these exploits of his were going to kill him, but would he listen?"

Ken said, "If I'd known he had heart problems, I would have done everything to stop him."

"I don't blame you, Ken. He'd have plowed ahead with or without you. None of us knew he had heart problems. I mean, I knew about the shortness of breath and even the occasional vertigo, but I chalked it up to us reaching our fifties." Mary sighed heavily.

Elliott said, "I guess him running up the stairs like that is what did it. Scary stuff."

A voice called out from a back bedroom. "I'm awake now, and I haven't gone deaf yet."

Mary grinned. "He's been grumpy like this for a week. Let's go back and harass him."

Elliott said, "Nothing I'd like better, after what he's put us through." He added a louder, "Hear that?"

Cameron said, "Come back here, if you dare."

Mary said, "Are you decent?"

"If being smothered under a ton of sheets and blankets is what you call decent, yeah."

Mary stood and beckoned the others to follow her to Cameron's 'recovery suite,' where he had propped himself up against the headboard, still covered head-to-toe with blankets. His emergency angioplasty had gone well, but he had doctor's orders to rest. Mary said, "Everybody wanted to see how you're doing. I told them that your stubbornness didn't kill you this time, but..."

Cameron said, "I kow, I know, I had warnings and I ignored them; it's as simple as that. You'd think that after a heart attack did my father in, I'd know better, but you know human nature–things always happen to everybody else, not us. So here we are."

Mary retrieved two pills and a glass of water from Cameron's nightstand, and gave them to him. "You got lucky this time, Boo. Your attack didn't kill you. Now, every time you're tempted to rush into one of 'those' cases, you can think about that stent and leave the heavy lifting to Ken, okay?".

Ken said, "Whoa. How 'bout we pass those cases on to somebody else from now on?"

Cameron laughed, but stopped abruptly, gasping. He still had not fully recovered from the operation. Elliott said, "Take it easy, cowboy, you still have about another week of bed rest to go. Let's not stretch it out any further."

Cameron, looking falsely contrite, pointed to Ken and Mary and said with a wan smile, "Their fault." The gasp having subsided, he continued, "I'm glad everybody's here to fill me in what happened. Last thing I remember, I got to the top of the stairs, felt really dizzy and disoriented, and then started stumbling around. After that? I don't know."

Ken said, "I don't know either. I got your text, zeroed in on catching Loretta, and didn't even see you passed out in the corner. Sorry."

"Oh hell, no need to apologize; that's what I asked you to do. So, who finally found me?"

Mary said, "A state trooper. I'm not sure what brought him up there, but he's the first person Ken and I saw. He said he'd talked to you on the loading dock or something."

"Oh yeah, the same one I warned about Loretta, I guess he took the hint after all. I'll have to send him a thank-you. Speaking of Loretta, I'm pretty sure she had a master key hanging from a coil bracelet on her wrist. I 'spect that's how she got through the stairway door. Think maybe Gus gave it to her?"

Elliott said, "No, Jerry Dale gave it to her. He stole it from Gus when he killed him. He told us that as part of his plea deal. He ordered Ms. Jackson to break into the auditorium with it to plant the bomb. She was lucky she did it right before Stevens changed the shop door lock."

"Dale ordered her to do it? What hold did he have over her?"

"Drug money."

"She comes from a decent family, so how'd that happen?"

"Somewhere along the line, she got mixed up with a bad crowd. They turned her on to an expensive drug habit that she couldn't afford. Then, when she got paired up with Jerry Dale in the band, it didn't take him long to catch on to her problems. He convinced her she could make some easy money, if she'd do what he said."

Mary shuddered and said, "Ugh, 'fun time' drug use turns into 'gotta have it' desperation in no time, doesn't it?

Cameron said, "You're right about that. I guess you never know what can make your kid take a wrong turn. And now she's..."

"Dead. Broken neck. The only reason George survived is because she cushioned his fall a little."

Ken said, "Elliott, did the bomb squad figure out what was in that bundle she grabbed?"

Cameron said, "Bundle?"

"Yeah. Remember when we looked up into the ceiling superstructure from the FOH rail?"

"Yeah. It was too dark up there for us to see much."

"That's where she hid the bundle of explosives, so we couldn't see it. When I got up there, George Hall tried to stop her from reaching it, they wrestled for it, she lost her balance, and they both went through the ceiling."

"Holy cow. And I missed all that."

Elliott said, "Bomb squad tells me the bundle was C4 explosive, probably enough to kill or maim the front half of the audience."

"Whew! I guess they were so bent on killing the governor, they didn't care about collateral damage, did they?"

Elliott said, "Nope. Luckily, the only collateral damage was a slew of arrests; Buck Randall, Oren Danford, and Jerry Dale, among others. Oh, and Jodie Miller. She helped plan it, too."

Cameron said, "No wonder she wanted to go home early."

Ken said, "That Dale. He's a piece of work. Did I hear right that he's related somehow to Buck Randall?"

Elliott said, "His stepson, yeah, but Randall pretty much treated him like dirt. Dale got wind that Randall and Oren Danford were plotting to eliminate Oren's brother, and he figured he could win stepdaddy's 'affection' by offering to help. The plot to bomb Graves Auditorium grew from that unholy alliance."

Mary said, "Unholy alliance is right. And they thought they'd get away with it?"

"Shoot, they planned to pin it on a group of really vocal anti-Danford extremists. Instead, they're all in jail now."

Cameron said to Elliott, "At least our efforts didn't completely go to waste. I read that Governor Danford was shocked and heartbroken to find out who was behind the plot, and thanked George Hall, along with you and Sergeant Crowley's security folks. I wish we'd have put it all together in time to save George and Loretta though."

Mary said, "I know you shy away from public mention when these things happen, Cameron, so I'm glad George got credit. Does anybody know how George got involved in all this in the first place?"

Elliott said, "I'm afraid we read him wrong. Turns out, he's distantly related to Randall, but hates him. Gus Danford worked with

-193-

Hall long enough to trust him, so he told him about the plot. I think that's why Jerry iced Gus. We jailed Dale before he could kill George. We found out that George wanted to warn us, but he figured that nobody'd listen to an ex-con."

Cameron said, "How's his recovery coming along?"

Elliott said, "Let's just say it'll take a hell of a lot longer than yours, buddy, much as he got busted up. He's up at Duke Hospital for some serious back surgery."

"Let's hope he comes through it well."

"Governor said he's going to get his record expunged and get him off parole."

"That's great."

Ken said to Cameron, "It shocked the hell out of me when you texted about Loretta. What brought her up on your radar?"

"Cameron said, "It's a little complicated; a lot of small clues came together at the last minute. George brought her to the edge of the screen when he told us about her and Dale talking."

"I remember that."

"Okay, you also remember when Dolores told us that her mother got a warning from somebody who signed the text with an 'L'?"

"Uh huh."

"You know about the screen name 'L Boom' for one of Jodie's correspondents. Paula couldn't find the name in time, but who do we know that 'booms' a lot?"

"Loretta on the timpani. Of course"

"Well, that fact rolled around in the back of my mind until it finally sprung a memory loose. Mary, you know my friend from Rotary, Henry Jackson?"

"The school principal?"

"That one. I remembered Henry bitching to me about one of his daughters having some 'problems.' He didn't elaborate, but said he was gonna have his long-time friend Sharon, who's a school drug counselor to work with the daughter. All this crap going on made me realize that Loretta was probably the 'problem' daughter and the counselor was probably Sharon Taylor. Elliott, what you just told me bears that out."

Cameron Paused to take a few breaths, and then continued, "Obviously the intervention didn't work but, but I think that over the course of counseling, Loretta grew fond of Sharon. That's why she sent her a warning–so she wouldn't get hurt when the bomb went off."

Mary said, "A tinge of compassion in the middle of all that hate. Wow"

"Exactly. And yet, we found out that Loretta's the one who suggested to Katherine that she invite her uncle to the concert. Of course, now we know why."

"Quite a contradiction, for sure."

"The next clue came from her, when she told Ken and me that Jerry Dale and Chip Eason were good buddies who made trouble in the band together. Yet Eason said that he and Dale barely knew each other and each made trouble in their own way. Evidently, she lied to steer me toward them as troublemakers and away from her."

Elliott said, "I didn't know that."

"You or Ken, neither one, knew about her trip out to the loading dock at intermission, supposedly to have a smoke. But I remembered that when I talked with her at my office, and even backstage that evening, she didn't have any tell-tale smoker's odor on her clothes. And, when I went out on the dock to check on her, the trooper who was supposed to be guarding the door was out there smoking, but she wasn't. All of those incidents clicked together to tell me that something was going to happen, and that she wanted an excuse to be outside when it did."

Elliott said, "Smoking certainly was hazardous for her health, wasn't it?"

The pills that Mary had given to Cameron started to take effect and his eyelids started to droop. He fought the drowsiness long enough to comment to Elliot, "You know, I'm still not sure how 'The Old North State' figures into this."

Elliott explained, "Randall's twisted mind came up with the idea to set off the C4 when the state song played, so Dale made a trigger that coupled some kind of newfangled 'smart' device for the music industry with a timer. The song's three-quarter tempo would set it off, but the timer would keep it from detonating during rehearsal. Thing is, Dale was smart enough to come up with all that, but too dumb to use a good battery; It was nearly dead before the concert started. Randall thought that using the state song as a trigger provided a nice touch of irony."

Mary said, "How ironic that it provided Randall's undoing."

Cameron managed a faint laugh, but his eyes were drooping heavily. He blinked off the drowsiness one more time, and asked Ken," How's Ben holding up to the extra work? In fact, how are you holding up?"

Ken said, "Don't worry about us. You keep mending, and we'll keep the office going. By the way, Mia says 'hey'. She wanted to be here tonight, but she had to work late."

"I appreciate the work you two and Ben been doing. And tell Mia I said 'hey' back. Well, looks like you've got another escapade under your belt, pal."

By this time, Cameron's eyes were nearly shut, and Mary said, "Thanks to you both for coming, but he's probably had enough fun for tonight." She saw Elliott and Ken to the door and came back to the bedroom.

Mary pulled a chair close to the bed, where Cameron's left hand rested above the blankets. She took it in hers, saying "You've had some mighty close calls with all your escapades, but I think they'll quiet down now, for a long time to come, right?" She squeezed his hand tightly, to the point that he winced. "Right?"

With a half grimace, half smile, he said, "Right. Now please ease off."

Mary eased her grip, smiled warmly, and said, "You need to rest now–go to sleep. She kissed his forehead as he drifted off. Under the blankets, two fingers of his right hand were still crossed.

THE END

Made in the USA
Columbia, SC
01 September 2024